Riddle
in the
Mountain

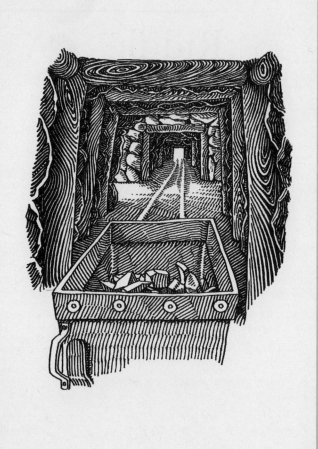

Riddle
in the
Mountain

Daryl Burkhard

With illustrations by
Frank Riccio

Dogtooth Books
Fort Collins, Colorado

For my nieces,
Elizabeth Marie Burkhard
and
Katherine Cain Burkhard

While the historical settings and a few of the characters in this book are based on actual places and real people, the story itself, including the main characters and their adventures, are works of fiction, created by the author. For an overview of what is real and what is invented, see the historical notes beginning on page 234.

Text © 2005 Daryl R. Burkhard. All rights reserved.
Illustrations © 2005 Frank Riccio. All rights reserved.

Cover design: Mayapriya Long / Bookwrights
Interior design: Deborah Robson

Publisher's Cataloging-in-Publication provided by Quality Books, Inc.

Burkhard, Daryl.
   Riddle in the mountain / Daryl Burkhard ; with illustrations by Frank Riccio.
   p. cm.
   SUMMARY: Three children, transported to 1879, must solve a mystery involving Cornish folklore, magic and the mining-era of the American West before they can return home.
   Audience: Ages 9–12.   LCCN 2005924733   ISBN 0-9668289-5-X

   1. Time travel—Juvenile fiction.   2. Boulder (Colo.)—History—Juvenile fiction.   [1. Time travel—Fiction.   2. Boulder (Colo.)—History—Fiction.   3. Mines and mineral resources—History—Fiction.]   I. Riccio, Frank   II. Title.

PZ7.B92287Rid 2005   [Fic]
                                           QBI05–800258

ISBN-13: 978-0-9668289-5-5 (hardcover)
ISBN-10: 0-9668289-5-X (hardcover)

Nomad Press participates in the Green Press Initiative and contributes a percentage of its resources to non-profit organizations working on projects related to the topics of its books.

Printed in Canada
Distributed to the trade by National Book Network

Dogtooth Books

an imprint of
Nomad Press
PO Box 484   10 9 8 7 6 5 4 3 2 1
Fort Collins CO 80522-0484 USA   www.nomad-press.com

Contents

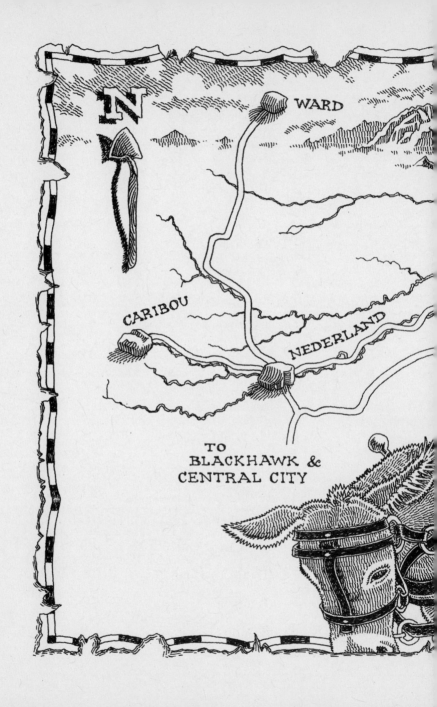

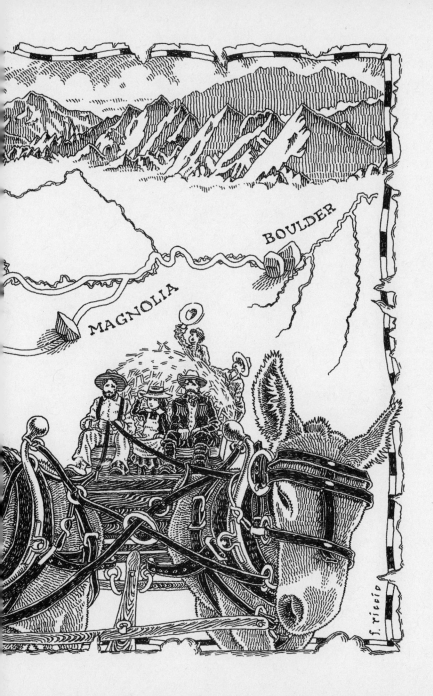

MAGNOLIA

BOULDER

f. riccio

1   A Voice in the Dark

It wasn't the wind that woke Kathy Henley in the middle of the night or the scratching of twigs at the window. With eyes wide and alert, she huddled against the headboard of her bed and pulled the covers close to her chin. She could swear she had heard a voice in the dark. Just a whisper. Calling.

She peered about the moonlit room, searching every shadow and hidden corner. Her gaze slid across the flowers adorning her chest of drawers and drifted past the chair with tomorrow's clothes folded neatly over the back. It rested momentarily on the crowded bookcase, where her sketchpad and box of pencils snuggled next to a picture of Grandmother Faye.

Kathy couldn't see her grandmother's face in the dark, her thick silver hair, or the chain necklace she always wore. It didn't matter. Kathy knew the face well. It was much like her own. The same square chin and moss-colored eyes. And when her grandmother was young, the same flame-red hair. Kathy didn't remember her grandmother, young or old, but everyone said they were a lot alike.

Kathy whispered a tiny prayer to the darkened photo, hoping her grandmother might hear. As if in answer, a sigh brushed through the open window and rustled the draperies. Startled, Kathy scrunched smaller. She scanned the room, again—once, twice—then eased out of bed and onto the floor. On tiptoes, she dashed to the bathroom, rushed through to the bedroom on the other side, and pounced on her brother's bed.

"David," she hissed, shaking the lumpy body under the bedspread. "Wake up!"

A moan escaped from the quilted mound as it rolled, turned, and then settled again into the steady rhythm of a soft snore. Waking David was like waking the dead.

No, Kathy thought as she stared back toward her bedroom. In this house, the dead woke up more easily.

Well, maybe.

This *was* her first week in Boulder, Colorado. She didn't know the routine night noises of the three-story brick

house her family now called home. But the sound she had heard was no creak of wood or clunk of household appliance, and she had felt a quiver run up her spine— the same quiver she sometimes felt in cemeteries.

"David," she hissed again, shaking him one more time. "Wake up!"

The snores subsided to a heavy breathing, but still her brother slept.

Kathy knelt on the floor, hugged her chest, and leaned against her brother's bed. She hated feeling afraid, hated hearing things that weren't there. In one more day she would be twelve, so why was she such a baby?

She already knew in the morning the sun would be bright, the memories would fade, and the rest of her family would chuckle at what they called her overactive imagination. But knowing that didn't help. Now, no matter what she told herself, she was sure there was something there in the dark. She didn't want to be alone.

She shook her head, angry with herself. She had to stop being afraid. She glanced at the lump that was her thirteen-year-old brother, then back at the bathroom and the darkness beyond. Maybe, if she could just— turn on the light?

Riding a wave of momentary courage, she pushed herself off the floor and scrambled toward the bathroom. Halfway there, she tripped over a pile of shoes and jeans.

She fell against the wall with a crash and crumpled against David's flimsy bookcase. Several rocks and a battered soccer ball tumbled to the floor. If there *was* anything in the dark, it knew where to find her now.

In a panic, Kathy reached around the corner and slapped her hand on the wall, searching for the light. She found the switch and flicked it up. A soft yellow beam flooded the bathroom and overflowed into the bedrooms. Quickly, she slipped into its glow, leaned against the wall, and sighed. Then she stared at her reflection in the mirror, wondering what the pale, freckle-faced phantom with the flyaway hair would do next.

"What's going on?"

Kathy shrieked and spun around, nearly hitting her brother.

"Ow," he said. "You yelled right in my ear." He rubbed the side of his head and frowned. "You made enough noise to wake the dead. What did you do? Run into the wall?"

Kathy glared up at her brother. He towered over her, in rumpled pajamas. He was tall for his age: thin and athletic, a star on his old school's soccer team. He never ran into anything. She, on the other hand, was short and clumsy, forever tripping over and into things. It didn't help that she still carried her baby fat. "You'll grow out of it, dear. It just takes time," her mother had said. Kathy figured that meant never.

"What's going on?" David repeated, blinking into the light.

"I heard something," she replied, nervously rubbing her hands on the baggy T-shirt that hung to her knees. She wondered how much to share. "I got scared," she finally added.

David uttered a disgusted grunt. "You always get scared. Probably made the whole thing up. You heard night noises. That's all."

"I did not," Kathy snapped, angry that David wouldn't listen. "I heard a voice and I got that funny feeling, too."

"Right," her brother snorted, scratching at sleep-tousled hair. "You feel funny all the time. Mom says it's puberty. I think you're nuts." Shaking his head, he turned toward his bed.

"But David—"

"Get over it," he said, with a wave of his hand. "Go back to bed." He stopped, twisted his head around, and gave her a warning look. "But not in *my* room." He turned back around, kicked his clothes out of the way, and crawled into bed. "And turn out the light," he added as he rolled over and pulled the covers over his head.

Muttering under her breath, Kathy flipped off the light and stomped into her room. Halfway to the bed, her steps slowed to a stop. Her gaze again darted from one dark corner to the next. She still didn't want to be alone.

Feeling as if she were back in preschool, she grabbed her pillow and tugged the covers off her bed. Balling the blanket up in her arms, she hurried through the large room that served as a hallway and slipped into her parents' bedroom on the other side of the house. Her father's snores rumbled in the air, mingling with the soft wheeze of her mother's breath.

Careful not to disturb her parents, she plopped her bedding on the floor between their king-size bed and the two corner windows facing south and east. She pushed the pillow up against the wall and folded the blanket into a makeshift bed. As she lifted the top flap to crawl underneath, a whisper floated through the air, calling. Kathy froze, a tingle prickling up and down her spine.

The whisper was louder this time. She could almost hear words and. . . . Kathy turned to face the windows. She'd swear it came from outside.

Hands trembling, she reached for the window sill and slowly peeked over its edge. A jumbled collage of shadows and moonlight greeted her as the sharp profiles of brick and stone houses cut through the softer edges of trees and shrubs. Mapleton Hill was an old neighborhood. No two houses were alike. Some loomed large and elegant, while others nestled modestly nearby. All the houses were dark. All except one.

Inside the small stone house next door, a lamp glowed, brightening curtained windows and spilling light out the open front door. On the porch, a short, old woman stared into the night, tense and alert as if listening.

Kathy watched, mesmerized, wondering who this person was and why she was awake in the middle of the night. Did she hear the whisper, too? Or was she the one who was calling? The woman stood, unmoving, for what seemed like an eternity, until, at last, she turned to go inside. As she reached for the open door, she looked up toward Kathy and smiled.

Kathy ducked. Did her neighbor know she was here? Could she see through the window in the dark? Kathy crouched against the wall, wondering what to do. Then she shoved her pillow closer to her parents' bed and crawled between the blanket folds. Pulling the cover high over her head, she waited for morning.

2 The Challenge

Kathy scowled as she rubbed at the sketchbook in her lap, scattering bits of eraser to the ground five feet below. As expected, the day had arrived bright and beautiful, mocking her fears. And, as in the past, her parents and brother had poked fun at her night escapade. With a flourish, David imitated the terrified shriek in the bathroom, while her father recounted how he had almost stepped on her as he got out of bed. Everyone had a good laugh. Everyone—except Kathy.

Despite the sun and cheerful light, an echo of the voice still whispered in her head. She still couldn't make out the words. And what *was* the voice anyway? Her neighbor? Something else? If she had been in Virginia, she could have talked it over with her best friend Sharon, but here she had no friends, no one to talk to who wouldn't laugh.

She shifted her position on the sandstone wall that wrapped around the backyard, then squinted at the Douglas fir, silver maple, and chestnut tree that cloaked her secluded spot. The chestnut tree on her paper was half-formed, its trunk rough and wide. She traced a thick line with her pencil to darken a knot in the wood, then leaned closer to inspect her drawing. A face, craggy with age, seemed to peek out of the bark. A face with beady eyes and a large bulbous nose. That was not what she had intended.

She picked up the eraser to scrub away the nose, then started as a loud *slam* cracked through the air. Twisting around, she peered through the leaves of her neighbor's apple tree and watched a stocky, gray-haired woman stroll from the stone house toward an enormous flower garden. A stained smock covered the woman's calico dress and a wide-brimmed straw hat shadowed her wrinkled face. The woman stopped, turned her head, and looked directly at Kathy.

"Katherine Faye. What are you doing, sitting there like a little mouse?"

Kathy dropped her eraser in surprise. It bounced off the top of the wall and tumbled to the ground. Kathy let it lie. "You know my name!"

"Naturally. I know all of my neighbors," the woman said. "I am Eleanor Acheson. Mrs. Acheson will do. Come down, child," she said with a wave. "Come help me with my flowers."

Kathy hesitated, but the flower bed was tempting with its sweet perfume drifting in the air. Ignoring the stray eraser, she set her sketchbook aside and swung her legs over the wall. Holding onto the top, she eased herself down—until her foot slipped, banging her right knee into the stone and loosening her grip. She fell to the ground with a *thump*.

Mrs. Acheson shook her head and chuckled, emerald-green eyes twinkling in the morning light. "Not the Queen of Grace, are you, dear?" she said. "Never you mind. Come along. The flowers are cheerful this morning."

Humming, she waded into the splash of color that filled her yard, her laced, leather ankle boots gently pushing tender plants aside. Reds, yellows, pinks, and purples bobbed in her wake like birds floating on a rainbow sea. Now and then, Mrs. Acheson stopped to whisper to a flower, stroking its face. A sharp scolding, followed by the snatch of a gloved hand announced the presence, and end, of a weed.

Kathy pushed herself off the ground and watched her neighbor navigate the garden. She couldn't help but grin. Mrs. Acheson reminded her of a puttering old gnome pictured in one of her storybooks. Enchanted by the image, Kathy stepped into the rippling color.

Mrs. Acheson waved her on. "Come look at my foxgloves," she said, bobbing her head toward a mass of bell-shaped flowers that hung like yellow chimes on slender stalks. "The fairies love the purple ones best," she added, "but those only bloom in the spring." Not noticing the startled look on Kathy's face, she turned toward a patch of pink flowers. "And these are fairy slippers." She picked one of the slipper-shaped blossoms and handed it to Kathy. "Have you ever heard the fairies dance at night and wondered where they get their shoes?"

Kathy blinked, unsure what to think, then slowly shook her head.

"Neither have I," Mrs. Acheson sighed, pushing wisps of hair out of her face. "But Lord, I keep trying. Now, if I had the gift, it would be different. Ah, look, another weed." She bent down and twisted the offender out of the ground, then tossed it aside.

Kathy studied the flower in her hand, twirling it between her fingers. She wondered if her neighbor was a bit daft. That might explain the whisper. "Was that what you were doing last night?" she asked. "Talking to fairies?"

Mrs. Acheson smiled. "I thought I felt someone watching. No, dear. Not talking. Listening. And it wasn't fairies. I heard something else—a restlessness in the wind. It comes every first week in July. I can never quite make it out. It's like. . . ." She bowed her head in thought and frowned.

"Was it . . . a whisper?" Kathy asked, so softly she didn't know if her neighbor would hear.

Mrs. Acheson's head snapped up. "You heard a voice?"

Kathy stepped back, surprised by her neighbor's sharp tone. She started to answer, but stopped as a loud crash cut through the air.

"Ow," a boy cried from behind the back fence. "You almost broke my hand."

"I didn't mean to," another said. "The lid's heavy."

Kathy gaped at the familiar voice, and almost cried out a warning as Mrs. Acheson bolted toward the alley. Instead, she ran after her neighbor. With amazing speed, the woman reached the gate, swung it open, and snatched at the boy standing there. Kathy's brother let out a startled cry and dropped the lid to the concrete incinerator—right on top of another boy who was rummaging in the pit.

"Ow," the boy bellowed. "Get this thing off me."

Mrs. Acheson released her grip on David and yanked up the metal lid. A tall, lanky boy scrambled to his feet and slapped at his sand-colored hair. "You could have killed me," he complained, as dark specks of soot flittered down and settled onto his freckled face.

"Serves you right," Mrs. Acheson snapped. "What are you doing in my trash?"

The boy hunched his shoulders and glanced at David, who stood straight as a pole, looking mortified.

"We're hunting for stuff," the boy said, warily. He reached down and picked up a tarnished, antique-looking bowl. "Old stuff. Like this." His scowl lifted as excitement washed over his face. "I bet this is over a hundred years old and if we polish it up, it'll look just like new."

Mrs. Acheson reached out, took the bowl, and turned it over. She shook her head and *tsked*. "A reproduction, no more than ten years old. See that date?" She pointed to the bowl's bottom, then handed it back. Disgusted, the boy tossed the worthless object into the concrete bin.

Mrs. Acheson frowned. "Aren't you the Kessler boy, Frank?" she said, eyeing him up and down. "And you, young neighbor," she added, poking at David, "you're getting off to a bad start. You boys won't find anything in my incinerator. It hasn't been used in years." She crossed her arms and scrutinized the guilty pair, then pointed toward the gate. "Inside," she said.

David and Frank exchanged worried looks. Frank jammed his hands into the tattered pockets of his jeans, refusing to budge, while David glanced anxiously about as if looking for an escape. When he saw Kathy standing by the wooden fence, he groaned in resignation, and shuffled toward the gate. Frank didn't move—until Mrs. Acheson stepped toward him, drawing her short frame up until she looked surprisingly menacing. Then, dragging his feet, Frank followed David.

Single file, the boys trudged into the backyard. David led the way, his face clouded with frustration and, Kathy suspected, a little fear. Behind him, Frank plodded along, staring at the ground, until he almost bumped into Kathy. Startled, he looked up. His eyes widened briefly, then narrowed into a cocky glare. He opened his mouth to speak, but Mrs. Acheson poked him with a finger and prodded him on. Waving her charges forward, she marched them to the garden's edge, then ordered them to halt.

"If you two rascals have time to pry into other folk's trash, then you have time to help me," she said, ignoring the sour looks on the boys' faces. "There are weeds in my garden. I could use young backs and deft hands. You can start there." She pointed toward the fairy slippers. "Be careful. I don't want a single flower harmed."

"But," Frank protested. "We don't have time. I mean—"

"Do I need to speak to your parents?" Mrs. Acheson asked, cutting him off.

David groaned and dropped to his knees. With soot-stained fingers, he rooted through the pink blossoms, searching for errant weeds. Eyeing Mrs. Acheson, Frank knelt beside him and picked up a digging stick. Kathy grinned. She couldn't help but feel smug, not after the morning's teasing. Frank didn't seem to appreciate her humor. Scowling, he yanked at a patch of crab-grass. Then, with his stick, he slashed at the remaining blades.

"Killing it once is enough," Mrs. Acheson said, before turning her attention toward Kathy. "Now, what about a whisper?"

The smile evaporated from Kathy's face. Already she could see David rolling his eyes as he plucked out a dandelion. Frank's hand stopped mid-air.

"It's nothing really," she said quickly, hoping to avoid the subject. "The foxgloves are nice, aren't they, David? And look, there's another dandelion."

David sat back on his heels, the devil's grin on his face. "Kathy thinks our house is haunted," he said. "She thinks she heard a voice last night."

"A voice?" Mrs. Acheson asked eagerly. "A voice with words?"

"I—I think so," Kathy stammered, surprised by the question—surprised Mrs. Acheson took her seriously. "I couldn't really make them out."

"Oh, get real," David said to his sister. "Some old branch scratched at the window and scared you." He turned toward Mrs. Acheson. "She does this all the time. Hears things that aren't there."

Kathy felt her face turn hot, especially when Frank twisted around and snickered in her direction. She wanted to bop David on the head and tell him to shut up.

Mrs. Acheson looked like she might do it for her. "How do *you* know something's not there?" the woman asked, glaring sharply at David.

"Well, of course nothing's there. I mean, I don't ever hear it and I've got better hearing than her. Besides, there's no such thing as ghosts. It's all just make-believe. Everybody knows that."

"Don't be so sure," Mrs. Acheson scolded, wagging her finger. "There are many worlds besides this one, worlds with allies, friends, and foes. But the doors to them are closing. Unbelievers—like you—slam them shut. And one by one the keys are lost." She placed her hands on her hips and looked around the yard. "What will we do when the need arises? What if the keys aren't found?" She slowly shook her head. "If only I had the gift."

David scrunched his face in disbelief. "You don't really believe that, do you? I mean, have you ever seen a ghost?"

"A ghost?" Mrs. Acheson scoffed, brushing a speck of dirt off her smock. "Ghosts are of *this* world. They belong to men. It's the others I'm concerned about. Have I seen them? No—only shadows, I think. How can I? Most doors are closed now, and I don't have the key. Or the gift to wield it. But Great-grandfather Penhallow did. And he saw tommyknockers."

"Saw what?" Frank asked. He no longer seemed concerned with Kathy, or the bindweed dangling between his fingers.

"Tommyknockers," Mrs. Acheson replied. "Little old men who live in the mines. Dwarves, some folks call them, but they're not. Great-grandfather was a miner, you see. He worked the silver mines in Caribou before he died. Tommyknockers know the mountains. They know where the rich veins are. And sometimes," she said, looking pointedly at David and Frank, "sometimes they would tell Great-grandfather." She clasped her hands together and chuckled. "That made him a popular man with some folks—and," she added, frowning, "the envy of others."

"You've got to be kidding," David said.

"Absolutely not."

"But, then wouldn't you be rich? I mean, he'd find all that silver, right?"

Mrs. Acheson prodded a tiny thistle in the ground with the toe of her shoe. "No, not really," she replied. "I don't think the gift is meant for personal gain. Great-grandfather tried once . . . and paid dearly." She rubbed her hands on her smock and looked oddly over at Kathy. "The gift is a tricky thing. It's not wise to let the world know you have it." She hesitated a moment, then continued. "Tell me, dear. Were you born with a caul?"

David grunted in surprise. Kathy simply stared. How did her neighbor know? Kathy had heard a million times how she had been born, half-wrapped in the birth sac, and how Grandmother Faye had fussed, insisting Kathy be called Faye, too.

Mrs. Acheson studied Kathy's face, then nodded. "As I thought," she said. She turned toward the boys with a baleful glare. "Thirty minutes, you two. Not a minute less." Smiling at Kathy, she added, "We'll talk later, dear." Without another word, she bent down, pulled up the battered thistle, then strode into the small, stone house.

"Batty old loon," David hissed under his breath as the door slammed shut.

Frank tossed the bindweed to the ground. "What was *that* about?"

"Oh, be quiet," Kathy snapped. She felt unsettled, even frightened by this strange new neighbor, and yet . . . Mrs. Acheson also had heard something last night. Someone finally believed her.

"What's the matter?" Frank said with a sneer. "You believe in ghosts? You get scared?"

"I do not get scared," Kathy shot back. Her brother didn't try to stifle his laugh.

"Your face is as red as your hair," Frank scoffed. "You are *too* scared."

"I am not."

"You are."

"Am not."

Frank leered up at Kathy, a grin spreading over his face. "If you're so brave," he said, "then let's go to the Elberts' house. They've got a ghost there, under the porch."

"Yeah, right," Kathy said. Her stomach flip-flopped despite her defiant voice. She felt queasy and wished she could go back to the seclusion of her trees. Where did David find this boy, anyway? She took a deep breath to hide her feelings, then jutted out her chin. "A ghost under a porch? How dumb can you get?"

This time David snorted at Frank. "It does sound kind of lame."

Surprise flickered across Frank's face before darkening into anger. "If it's so dumb, then let's find out." He poked David with an elbow. "Want to go ghost hunting? We can go tonight—unless your *sister's* scared."

Kathy held her breath. She didn't want to go, not ever. But she didn't dare say so. She watched David draw circles in the dirt with a finger as he mulled over his decision. Then, grinning, he looked up.

"Why not? But let's do it right. Let's go at midnight."

Kathy could have killed him. There was no graceful way to back out now. And David knew it. He knew she was afraid of the dark. He knew she was afraid of ghosts. And at midnight, it was her birthday. What kind of present was that? Fighting a rising panic, she glowered at her brother. Then anger flared up and burned away her fear.

"Fine," she said, squaring her shoulders. "Midnight. The three of us."

Frank grinned. "Yep," he said. "Tonight, we go ghost hunting!"

3 Under the Porch

Half-hidden under the blankets of her bed, Kathy turned her head toward David's room, listening. With any luck, she would hear the soft rhythm of snores rather than the busy stirrings of her brother getting dressed. Asleep, he would miss the midnight escapade. And if he didn't go, she didn't have to, either. With both hands, she crossed her fingers.

A tiny creak pulled her attention to the tall wooden wardrobe in the corner of her room. The closet doors were shut. She always closed them at night. No matter how old she was, how logical she tried to be, she couldn't help but feel that strange creatures lurked behind the portals waiting to sneak out. She thought of the porch and what might dwell beneath. Why ever did she agree to go?

She stared back at the bathroom door. To her dismay, a soft rustling floated from David's room, followed by muffled muttering. She groaned at the plop of shoes treading on the bathroom tile. David's head poked around the corner.

"It's time," he said, grinning like a Cheshire cat in the night.

"All right," she grumbled, throwing off the bedspread and blankets. "Go away while I get dressed."

In the dark, she pulled on the jeans and long-sleeved T-shirt draped over her chair. She slipped on socks and sneakers, then turned toward the closet doors. She didn't want to push them open. But she really had no choice. Squaring her shoulders and taking a deep breath, she shoved the right-hand door aside, fumbled for her faded denim jacket, then hurried toward the bedroom door.

David was waiting in the hallway. Like Kathy, he wore blue jeans and tennis shoes, topped with his favorite T-shirt, the one with their uncle's smokejumpers logo on the front.

"Hurry up," he whispered, slipping on his black nylon jacket and pulling up the zipper.

"Shh," Kathy whispered back.

They tiptoed down the stairs to the first floor hallway, where David twisted the brass handle of the front door. With a loud click and high-pitched squeak, the door swung open. Grimacing at the sound, Kathy stepped through the door onto the wooden porch. She waited while David closed the door behind them, then together they hurried down the flagstone sidewalk to the front gate.

"It's about time," Frank said, as he stood by the

spiked wrought-iron fence that guarded the front yard. Impatiently, he shifted from one foot to the other, hands stuffed deep into his jeans pockets. "I thought you'd chicken out," he said to Kathy with a smirk.

"You wish," she shot back. She charged through the gate, then had to stop. She didn't know which way to go.

Grinning, Frank brushed past her. "This way," he said.

His lanky legs stretched into long, brisk strides as he led them down the street. David marched beside him, matching pace for pace, while Kathy had to shift to a walk-trot in order to keep up.

They headed west toward the mountains, past the old elementary school where deep shadows slunk around corners and skulked behind large, drooping trees. The empty sandstone building with its newer brick additions made Kathy nervous in the dark. She was glad Frank kept to the grassy median that divided the quiet street. They walked block after block, always due west, until Frank abruptly turned south. He ambled a few more blocks, then stopped.

"Here it is," he said, waving at a house on a corner.

A large, two-story structure sprawled before them, partially hidden behind scraggly bushes and a tall spruce tree. Up and down the building's sides, dark-colored shingles cast a motley pattern of shadows, giving it an unkempt look compared to the clean brick lines of the other houses. Kathy barely noticed. It was the porch that caught her eye. It stood three feet high off the ground, spreading along the front and one side of the house. Wrapped around it, a thick, sandstone wall enclosed the crawl space underneath, while tall, white beams shouldered the roof above like pale square specters keeping watch.

Kathy shifted uneasily and moved closer to David.

"I guess we better check it out," he said.

He didn't sound eager. No one took the first step. The three of them stood there, arms crossed or hands jammed into pockets, as they stared at the house. Finally, David turned and faced the others.

"Hey," he said with a shrug and a grin, "there's no such thing as ghosts, remember?" With a look of determination, he stepped forward and strode toward the porch steps.

"Wait," Frank called after him in a half-whisper. "Not there. Over here."

He moved to the far end of the porch and into the shadows behind a clump of bushes. "In here," he said. "Come on." He waved for Kathy and David to follow. Kathy hesitated, preferring to stay on the sidewalk but knowing that then she would be left alone. Slowly, she crossed the yard and stepped around the bushes. There, in the middle of the sandstone wall, a small door of weathered, wooden planks hung slightly ajar, its rusty latch broken. Frank reached for the splintery wood and pulled. A dark hole opened up.

"How are we going to see?" Kathy whispered.

Frank grinned as he pulled a small silver cylinder from the inside pocket of his jacket. "Flashlights," he said as he clicked the light on and flicked it into Kathy's eyes.

"Stop it," she said, slapping at his arm.

He giggled, his voice cracking into a squeak.

"Knock it off," David said. "Let's go."

One by one, they crept under the porch, hands and knees scraping through the powdery dirt that carpeted the ground. Dank, stale dust billowed up, coating their mouths and noses with the taste and smell of dark, dead spaces. Frank led the way, flashing the light back and forth. David followed, with Kathy crawling behind. She didn't mind being last. After all, if there *was* something there, it would certainly get Frank first.

"Oh, man," Frank groaned. He flipped the light erratically from wall to ceiling to ground and back.

"What?" David whispered.

"Spider webs. I hate spider webs. What if there're black widows down here?"

"This was your idea," David replied.

"And you liked it," Kathy grumbled, as she moved away from the crevices along the walls, where she now imagined whole families of shiny black spiders with red hourglass markings on their bellies.

She crept forward, half-seeing, half-feeling her way. When they came to a sharp turn in the porch, they turned, too, and kept going until they reached the far back wall. By then, Kathy's heart was pounding so hard she could feel the throbbing in her ears.

"Okay, we came. Nothing here. Let's go home," she said, each word racing one after the other.

"No way!" Frank sounded bolder now that they were away from the spider webs. "Now we sit and wait."

"How long?" David asked. "It's awfully dusty down here. Pretty quiet, too. What are we supposed to see anyway?"

"I don't know," Frank answered. "I've never done this before."

"Great," David said. "We're down in the middle of a bunch of spiders and you don't even know if anything's here?"

"Everyone says there is," Frank retorted. "You think ghosts just pop out at your convenience?"

"Shh," Kathy whispered. "You guys are going to wake someone up and get us into trouble." It had occurred to her that "someone" might be the ghost, but she quickly dismissed the idea. She smiled. Frank didn't know anything. He probably made the whole thing up. There weren't any ghosts.

Just then, a tiny sound, like nails in a metal bucket, rattled in the shadows behind her. She whirled around, bumping into David as he, too, twisted to stare down the tunnel.

"What's that?" he whispered.

Kathy crouched, unmoving, as she strained to hear. The nervous rasp of the boys' breath hissed behind her in the otherwise quiet air. Still, she felt a quiver run up her spine. Slowly she backed up, pushing into her brother.

"It—it's O.K.," he said. "Just a mouse—or something."

"Right," Frank whispered. "Just a mouse. No biggie."

A high-pitched giggle, ever so slight, tittered out of the darkness.

"Who disturbs my solitude, my banishment, my pain?" The wispy voice swirled like a restless wind in and out of the crannies along the sandstone walls.

"Oh, god," Frank moaned. The beam from his flashlight shook.

"David?" Kathy reached for her brother's hand and squeezed. He squeezed back even harder.

A chuckle bounced off the wooden ceiling as a small,

almost shimmery man stepped into the light. He stood just under three feet tall, his battered felt cap brushing the beams of the porch above. Coal-black eyes twinkled in the light while a large bulbous nose protruded from a face so wrinkled it reminded Kathy of finely cracked clay—or the rough-lined bark of a chestnut tree.

The little man scratched his long, gray beard with a large, oversized hand. "You can hear me," he said. "See me, too." He glanced around the poorly lit tunnel. "The door's been opened wide," he added with surprise. He stepped toward the trio, his heavy boots stirring up dust to coat his faded blue pants and sweat-stained shirt. "Did you hear me call through the crack last night? The door was almost shut. One of you pushed it open. One of you has the gift."

No one said a word. Kathy was too scared to speak.

The man crossed his arms and eyed them from under bushy brows. "One of you could save the key. Return it to its rightful place. Then I could go home." He sighed and shook his head, flashing large, pointy ears in the shivering light. "To feel the mountain stone again and taste the glimmering ore." He reached out to touch the air as if longing for something that wasn't there.

Suddenly a rifle-shot of laughter ricocheted against the sandstone walls. "You looking for adventure?" he asked, the sparkles in his eyes flashing brighter. "Then I shall give you mine." He stepped forward and pointed a gnarled finger at them. "Into your minds I sear a riddle, beginning, end, and then a middle. Until you solve this riddle's line, the world is changed from yours to mine." He clapped his broad hands together, the sound of his raucous laugh echoing against stone and wood. Then, before the laughter died, he stepped into a shadow and disappeared.

A piercing shriek pounded Kathy's ears. She couldn't tell if it was hers, Frank's, or David's. All three were screaming. Frank pushed David and Kathy aside as he bolted back toward the weathered door. Kathy plunged after him, with David close behind. She bumped her head against the ceiling and her hands against the walls in a darkness unbroken by the discarded flashlight. She pushed her way into the moonlit night, out onto the grass. She scrambled to her feet, gasping for air, and ran toward the street, only to stop and stare.

There was no street. There were no trees. Open grassland spread before her and rolled down the bluff to twinkling lights in the valley below. She spun around and found . . . nothing. No house. No porch. Just a craggy hole in a small rock outcropping.

4 The Riddle

"Where did it go? What's happening?" Frank whirled around in a circle as he looked first at the rock outcrop and then down at the lights.

Kathy couldn't catch her breath. A cold vise squeezed her chest, pressing down the fear that filled her lungs, tightened her throat, and threatened to jump out in a terrified scream.

"David?" she squeaked.

David's face was sheet-white in the moonlight. He stared at the craggy hole, mouth open and eyes full of disbelief. "This is not real," he said. "This can't be real. It can't." He turned toward his sister and shouted. "What did you do?"

"What?" Kathy gasped, blinking in surprise. She couldn't understand the question. "What?"

"You heard," David snapped. "The 'gift.' One of us has the gift. Who do you think *that* is? You! You, with your weird voices and strange feelings. And . . . and the caul and . . . Grandma Faye fussing after you all the time when you were little." His voice rose to a hysterical pitch. "It's all your fault," he yelled. "If it weren't for you, we wouldn't hear him; we wouldn't see him; WE WOULDN'T BE HERE."

Kathy flinched as each word sliced into her already terrified brain. "You're lying," she shouted back. "I don't have anything. I don't remember Grandma Faye and what's she got to do with this, anyway?" She clenched her hands into angry fists. "The voices aren't real, remember? You said so. Daddy said so. It's just my imagination."

"What do you call that?" David pointed to the outcrop.

A sob caught in Kathy's throat as she stared at the very real, very solid rocks. "I didn't do it," she shouted. "It's not my fault. I don't even know what the gift is and I didn't want to come anyway. He did." She pointed a finger at Frank. "It's all *his* fault."

"Me?" Frank said. "All I wanted to do was go ghost hunting. I didn't know you were a . . . a . . . what are you, anyway?"

"Oh, shut up," David said, kicking hard at a rock on the ground. "You don't know anything."

"And you do?" Frank replied. "Fine. What do we do now?"

David muttered something incoherent, then walked over to the rocks. He knelt before the hole. "We've got to go back. It's got to be a wormhole or something. If we go in, maybe we'll come out in Boulder again."

Kathy eyed the black cavity. She did not want to go inside. It was dark, it was scary, and there really was something lurking there. She crossed her arms and hugged them tight. "Can't we go down to the lights and ask?"

"Ask what?" David said dryly before poking his head into the hole again. "Where's your flashlight, Frank?"

"I think I dropped it," he replied, patting his pockets to no avail. "Maybe we should—"

David grunted in disgust. Then before Frank could finish, he slipped into the hole and disappeared.

"David!" Kathy cried, running to the rocks. She poked her head into the hole and called, "David?" There was no response. Uneasily she stepped back and looked at Frank, who fumbled irritably in his pockets as if still searching for the flashlight. She glanced back at the crevice. She couldn't bear to go inside. Keeping her distance from Frank, she decided to wait instead. She waited . . . and waited . . . and waited, until she couldn't stand it any longer. She stuck her head deeper into the opening and hollered. "David!"

"Ow," he replied, crawling out of the hole. "Right in my ear." He scrambled to his feet and rubbed the side of his head.

"What took you so long?" Frank grumbled.

"I got stuck," David replied. "It's just a bunch of rocks and a hole."

Frank snorted and sat down on the grass. "Guess that's not the way home."

"Got any better ideas?" David snapped.

"Stay put and wait. That's what you do when you're lost. Let's wait until morning. Then we'll have some light."

Kathy couldn't argue with that. Apparently, neither could David. Together they huddled against the rock, careful not to get too close to each other or to the crevice. Kathy took the position farthest from the hole, letting Frank and David buffer her from the thing that dwelt there. She squirmed uncomfortably, trying to stay dry, but moisture from the dew-dampened ground seeped into her jeans and tennis shoes, adding a clammy chill to the sharp prick of brush and broken stone.

She sat in silence, surrounded by the tiny rustling of creatures in the grass, the hooting of an owl, and the ghostly wail of coyotes that wavered closer as the night wore on. She listened hard, relieved that these were normal night noises. Not whispers. Not voices. Not a little old man with a cap on his head. Still, by the time dawn flickered in the sky, her eyes were sore and dry from staring into the shifting gray shadows.

"Cripes," Frank said as light trickled across the plains and bathed the mountains to the west with a pale pink wash. "We're still here."

"Of course, we're still here," David said. "We haven't moved."

"I mean we're still here, in Boulder," Frank replied. "Or where Boulder should be. See?" He pointed to giant slabs of flat, jagged rock that rose out of the earth and leaned against the mountain slopes. "It's the Flatirons. And look over there." He swung his hand toward a smaller set of rocks jutting along the foothills like spines along a dinosaur's back. "Red Rocks, just where they should be." He twisted around to look at the rock outcrop, the bluff, and then the valley below. "We haven't moved. It's just—Boulder's gone."

"If Boulder's gone, then what is that?" Kathy asked, pointing down the bluff.

Below, a hodgepodge of houses, churches, and shops lay scattered along a checkerboard grid of dirt roads. In the center of town, one- and two-story brick buildings nestled shoulder to shoulder with smaller wooden structures masked by tall, square false fronts. There wasn't a single car in sight. Instead, wagons loaded with boxes and large machinery lined the street. Men ran back and forth, hitching up teams

of horses and mules, while shouts, neighs, and brays filled
the air. Already, several wagons trundled slowly toward the
mountain, their cargos swaying back and forth.

Kathy shivered. Despite the moist brush of dawn, the
valley looked brown and brittle, except for a green strip
of shaggy trees following a winding creek and the small
patches of gardens accompanying the houses. There were
hardly any other trees, unless she counted the thin sticks
of planted saplings standing at attention along the streets,
like so many toy soldiers. Without trees, even the surrounding bluffs and rolling plains looked barren and flat.
To Kathy, the place felt desolate.

"I've been thinking," David said, "about that dwarf
or whatever he is. He said something weird. Something
about a riddle and changing the world. 'Into your minds
I sear a riddle, beginning, end, and then a middle. Until
you solve this riddle's line, the world is changed from
yours to mine.'" He turned toward Kathy and Frank. "I
think we have to solve the riddle."

"I've been thinking the same thing," Frank said. He
cleared his throat, then began to recite. "'Up to the No
Name he will flee, to seek and steal the missing key. Up
Boulder Canyon all choked with dust, he will pursue his
own gold lust. All script in bronze, he'll find the key, not
meant to satisfy man's greed. It opens more than just a
map; the Otherworld lies at its lap.'"

"Where did you get that?" Kathy asked. "That's not
what he said."

"It is so," Frank replied.

"It is not. He said, 'So find the man who owns the key, a gifted one who hears and sees. To save this man you may be late, but more's at stake than one man's fate. It is the key that you must save, don't let me take it to its grave. Bring it forth through time and space to put it in its rightful place.'" Kathy frowned. "I can't believe I remembered that. I can't memorize anything."

"Well, that explains it," Frank snorted, "because that's *not* what he said."

"You're both wrong," David said, waving his hands to silence them. "He said, 'Beware the man with a golden smile, whose heart is black and filled with guile. He'll steal a map from an honest man, through fire and smoke and sleight of hand. Incomplete, the map he'll find, and so he'll plan a blacker crime. To right a wrong and end my shame, follow this man who is to blame.'" David furrowed his brow in thought. "I don't think we can get back until we fix something."

Kathy stared at David. "What ever are you talking about?"

"What do you mean, what am I talking about? That's what he said."

"No, he didn't."

"No way," Frank added.

The three of them argued back and forth, each insisting they were right, until Kathy gave up under the weight of the louder voices and sat on the rocks to watch. As the sunlight shifted from pink to a cool morning yellow, an idea took seed in her head. The more she thought about it, the bigger it grew until she was sure she was right. She jumped off the rocks and danced impatiently around the arguing boys, trying to interrupt, until she stepped on a prickly pear cactus half-hidden in the short prairie grass.

"Ow," she bellowed. The arguing stopped.

She hobbled over to the rocks and examined the bottom of her shoe. She couldn't find a thorn despite the stinging in her toe. She put her foot down and looked up.

"What if we're *all* right?" she asked. "What if there *is* a beginning, end, and middle, and we each heard a different part?"

She was answered first by blank stares, then the slow dawning of comprehension.

Frank moved closer, a skeptical look on his face. "So, what comes first? Which one's the beginning?"

They took turns repeating the verses they had heard. They recited them in different orders, searching for a combination that made sense. Kathy had trouble remembering David's or Frank's, but her own burned brighter in her mind with each repetition. Finally, they decided David's verse came first, Frank's second, and Kathy's third. Together, they chanted the starting rhyme, then continued, each adding their own verse in its proper place, until the riddle was complete.

The Riddle

Into your minds I sear a riddle—
beginning, end, and then a middle.
Until you solve this riddle's line,
the world is changed from yours to mine.

Beware the man with a golden smile,
whose heart is black and filled with guile.
He'll steal a map from an honest man,
through fire and smoke and sleight of hand.
Incomplete the map he'll find,
and so he'll plan a blacker crime.
To right a wrong and end my shame,
follow this man who is to blame.

Up to the No Name he will flee
to seek and steal the missing key.
Up Boulder Canyon, all choked with dust,
he will pursue his own gold lust.
All script in bronze he'll find the key,
not meant to satisfy man's greed.
It opens more than just a map:
the Otherworld lies at its lap.

So find the man who owns the key,
a gifted one who hears and sees.
To save this man you may be late,
but more's at stake than one man's fate.
It is the key that you must save.

Don't let me take it to its grave.
Bring it forth through time and space
to put it in its rightful place.

Frank rubbed his hands through his sandy hair. "Now what?" he asked.

"We start at the beginning," David replied. "We look for the man with a golden smile." He turned to stare at the valley below. "And the place to start is down there."

5 Old Boulder

In the middle of the night, when surrounded by darkness, the small town's lights had looked warm and inviting. But now, in daylight, Kathy felt safer hovering by the stony crevice that once had been a door under a porch. She wasn't sure she wanted to go down there.

Beside her, David stretched his arms, back, and legs as if warming up for a soccer game, while Frank leaned against the rocks with shoulders slouched and hands stuffed in his pockets. He had an odd, speculative look on his face as he scanned the valley below.

"I'm ready," David said, giving his arms a final shake. "Let's go find the man." Without looking back, he marched down the slope, arms swinging by his side. Frank grunted in agreement and fell in step beside him. He glanced over his shoulder at Kathy, a taunting grin on his face.

"Coming?" he asked, before turning away.

Kathy stuck out her tongue. She took one last look at the crevice, then trudged down the slope after the boys. She picked her way carefully, avoiding the prickly pear cactuses, scraggly clumps of rabbit brush, and a prairie dog hole or two. Partway down, they had to jump an irrigation ditch that wound along the side of the bluff. David and Frank sailed over with ease. Kathy, on the other hand, missed.

Her left leg slipped into the gurgling water. The rushing current grabbed her foot and threatened to drag her in. Frantically, she clawed at the side of the ditch. Scratching palms and fingertips on sharp rocks and ragged brush, she pulled herself up the bank. With a heave, she hauled herself over the top, tripped, and tumbled onto dry ground.

"What a klutz," Frank said, his chest heaving as if he had just been running. He placed his hands on his hips and twisted his lips into a half-smile.

"Oh, be quiet," Kathy muttered. Ignoring the sting in her hands, she pushed herself off the ground, brushed her bruised and bloody palms on her jeans, and stomped down the bluff without saying another word. She heard a snort behind her, followed by the scuffing of shoes on the ground. Frank strode past, nearly bounding down the hill. He lurched to a stop beside David, who had been waiting on the dirt road below.

"What took you so long?" David asked, eyeing his sister's wet pants.

"What do you think?" she snapped, annoyed that David had not come to help and that Frank still had a smirk on his face.

David shook his head. "Really, Kath, sometimes I think we're not from the same family. It wasn't a big ditch."

"Big enough," Kathy said. "I almost made it."

David rolled his eyes. "Yeah, right. Come on. We've got work to do." He turned toward town and tramped down the road. Frank eased along beside him. With hands smarting and denim sticking to her leg, Kathy followed as best she could—a good five steps behind.

They passed scattered houses perched along the edge of the valley: some were two-story, box-like brick buildings set in flat, green yards; others were small wood-frame homes with pointed gables and trim front porches. Except for the brightly colored flower beds or the tangled green of vegetable gardens nestled in the yards, Kathy ignored the houses. After all, they looked like the homes in her neighborhood.

Instead, she focused on the center of town, where riders on horseback clip-clopped down the sunbaked streets and horse-drawn buggies jangled along, stirring up clouds of dust that caught in her throat. Neighs, brays, and the barking of stray dogs filled the air, along with church bells calling congregations to worship. Walking into town was like entering a Western movie set—except this appeared to be real.

"This is so cool," Frank said, his head bobbing up and down as he strained to see everything. "Look—a blacksmith shop. Do you think it's open?" He veered toward the building with C. M. WILLIAMS, BLACKSMITH written across the top.

David grabbed his sleeve. "No time. We've got to find the man with a golden smile. That's what the riddle said."

"I suppose," Frank said half-heartedly. He looked longingly at the shop. "I don't hear anything inside anyway, but it sure would be fun to see." His face brightened with a smile. "I saw this museum once with a blacksmith's shop. It had a monster bellows for pumping the fire and these really nasty-looking iron clasps and hammers and sharpening stones. I just wish I could see them used for real." He stuck his hands in his pockets and turned away from the shop. "So what are we looking for, anyway?"

"I don't know," David replied. "Someone with gold braces or something."

"I don't think they have braces here," Kathy said, watching a man across the street clad in a dark wool coat and pants. He paced up and down the boardwalk, tall leather boots thudding on the wooden planks, while he scratched a thick black beard. He stopped and pulled a gold watch from his vest pocket. A slender chain dangled from the timepiece to a buttonhole mid-way up his chest. He clicked open the top, glanced at the time, then shook his head as he slipped the watch back out of sight.

"Are you sure the riddle said *smile?*" Kathy asked,

puzzled she couldn't remember the first verse. "Maybe it meant a gold watch."

"It didn't say *watch*. It said *smile.*" David repeated his verse from start to finish—twice—and had begun a third time when Frank waved for him to stop.

"Okay, okay," Frank said. "It said *smile*—and we know we're looking for a man. For whatever that's worth," he added glancing about.

There seemed to be men everywhere, in dark coats, vests, and trousers—riding, walking, or just standing. Some wore tall boots, like the man with the watch, while others sported dressier shoes or heavy work boots. Almost all had faces furred with mustaches or full beards and every one of them wore a hat.

"This isn't going to be easy," Frank said.

David pushed his jacket sleeves partway up his arms. "Then let's get started," he said as he marched down the street.

Kathy quickly tired of checking the faces of the men she passed. None smiled or nodded a greeting, much less gave a golden smile. Instead they frowned at her. Even the women in their long, narrow-skirted dresses and form-fitting bodices *tsk*ed as they strolled by.

"Hooligans," one woman hissed, as she hurried her children past.

Her two little girls snickered, with a toss of the long ringlets that bounced beneath their petite straw hats. Flouncing their plaid, calf-length skirts, they stomped past Kathy in red, high-buttoned shoes that glared against the white of long stockings and lacy pantalets. The small boy, dressed all in black with high boots and knickers, stared wide-eyed while his mother dragged him by.

"Momma," he said, pointing a stick of orange rock candy at Kathy. "She's not wearing a dress." His mother scowled, told him to hush, and pushed him along. He glanced over his shoulder at Kathy, then stuck out a yellowed tongue.

Frank flicked Kathy's hair with his hand. "If you cut your hair, they'll think you're a boy, and then we won't get all those nasty looks." Grinning, he turned away and walked over to a nearby shop window.

Kathy clenched her fists, wishing she could splatter Frank with pea-sized balls of mud, the same way

some local boys had splattered carriages that morning using long, wispy willow sticks. Or maybe splat him with the manure that littered the street. If her brother hadn't brought him home. . . . Kathy looked around for David.

Half a block away, her brother hovered around a group of men, bobbing up and down, waiting for them to smile. She shook her head, wondering how he could keep it up. She had had enough of frowns and scowls, and now she was tired and hungry.

"Hey," Frank said, beckoning her to his side. "Look at these marbles. I don't think I've ever seen any like them."

Grudgingly, Kathy stepped beside him to see. He was looking into a shop window framed by signs advertising stationery, paints, and toilet soap. On the window counter, a small wooden box held twelve clear glass marbles. Each contained a tiny silver animal figurine. Kathy could identify a dog, a chicken, a cat, and a cow, but it was the wild birds that caught her attention. A wide-eyed owl and sharp-billed eagle stared out from their glassy cages, so real she thought they might take flight.

Frank nudged her elbow. "Look," he said, pointing to another box filled with marble spheres of swirling color: ambers, greens, blues, and reds. Each swirl was different and the marbles were not quite round, as if each had been made by hand. Next to them, in a larger box, wooden tops tumbled over each other, faint strips of color wrapping circles around their swollen middles.

"I bet that stuff is really old," Frank said, rubbing his hands together. "I wish I could buy one. It'd be a *real* antique." He pressed his fingers against the glass. Then, with a sigh, he dropped his hand and drifted down the walkway to pause at another window.

Keeping one eye on David, Kathy followed Frank along the uneven boardwalk, listening to his idle chatter. He gawked at iron and wooden gadgets in the hardware store, trying to guess what each piece was, and held his nose by the saloon, where the odor of stale beer and sweat leaked out despite closed and shuttered doors. They laughed at the drug store with its display of tinctures, tonics, and rheumatic pills. When they came to the grocery store, with its pans, jars, jugs, and crates crammed next to barrels full of flour, sugar, cucumbers, and beans, Frank's stomach growled loudly. Kathy had almost forgotten how hungry she was.

"Look," Frank said, as he nudged her and pointed at the grocery window. Taped to the glass, a page from THE BOULDER NEWS & COURIER announced the prices of canned goods, including peaches, oysters, blackberries, tomatoes, and beans. At the top, a date was written in bold print:

FRIDAY, JULY 4, 1879

"This is the greatest!" Frank said. "I always wanted to live in the Old West. And look! We're here!" He bounced up and down on the balls of his feet. "Hey, David," he hollered, waving his hand. He bounded down the block and across the street.

Kathy read the newspaper ad again. Friday, July 4th. Friday? She looked around at the closed shops and the townsfolk who appeared to be dressed in their best. She remembered the peal of church bells earlier that morning, calling worshippers together. Today was Sunday. Today was July 6th—her birthday. They had arrived in old Boulder the same day they had left, only more than a hundred years earlier.

Kathy stared down at her scraped hands and dirty clothes. She thought of all her useless birthday plans. Brushing away a bead of sweat that trickled down her face, she glanced at the disapproving looks still sent her way. She didn't want to be here. She didn't want to be glared at. She didn't want to be scared. More importantly, she didn't want to be alone.

"Wait up," she cried, hurrying after Frank.

She hopped down from the warped wooden planks of the boardwalk, careful to avoid a pile of rotting food and discarded trash. Wrinkling her nose at the smell, she slapped at the large black flies hovering above the garbage. One particularly nasty fly hovered around her hair as she moved quickly past, buzzing her face and dabbing tiny feet on her skin. Waving, she forgot to watch her step. With a sickening squish, her foot slipped in a pile of fresh manure and she landed on the ground with a *thud.*

"Eew," David said, eyeing the greenish-brown muck that covered Kathy's shoe and spattered her jeans. He stood on the boardwalk across the street, arms crossed in disgust. "Can't you watch where you're going?"

Kathy sat on the hard, parched ground biting her lip as tears stung her eyes. She was dirty. She was tired. She was hungry. And now she stank.

From behind her, a hand reached down and tapped her shoulder.

"Young lady, I do believe you are a mess."

6 Rocky Mountain Joe

Kathy expected to be greeted by another frown and scowling face. Instead, she looked up into the warm smile of a handsome man with wavy brown hair, a neatly trimmed mustache, and a pointed goatee. Behind him, the sunlight cast a soft golden hue at the edges of his long curls, except for the one dangling over his forehead. Kathy sucked in her breath.

"I slipped," she said, stating the obvious. She couldn't think of anything better. In fact, she had trouble thinking at all.

The man chuckled. "Yes, I'd say you did. Let me help you up." He reached down, clasped her hand, and pulled her to her feet. "I reckon that pile got the better of you today," he said with a twinkle in his eye. He released her hand, then frowned at the scratches on her palm and fingertips. His gaze flickered down at the soiled jeans.

"What's a young lady doing all mussed up in boy's clothing?" he asked, a puzzled look on his face. "Surely you know folks don't take kindly to such behavior."

"It's none of your business," David said, charging into the street. He pulled his sister away and planted himself between her and the stranger. "She's with us."

The man blinked in surprise, then squinted as he noted David's nylon jacket and tennis shoes.

"David," Kathy hissed. "What are you doing?" She didn't like being yanked around and shoved into the background—especially now. She elbowed her brother aside and stepped toward the man. David pulled her back and leaned toward her ear.

"He's smiling," he said between gritted teeth. He twisted around to hide his face from the stranger's view and cracked his lips in an exaggerated clown's grin. "You know, *smile?*"

"Oh," Kathy said. She looked up at the stranger. Could his charming smile be the golden smile? It *was* the only smile they had encountered all day and there *was* a golden glow about him. Still, she didn't think that was what the riddle meant. Apparently, neither did Frank.

"Do you know where we can get some food?" Frank asked loudly, as he sauntered over to join them.

David jabbed Frank sharply in the ribs, urging him to be quiet.

"No," Frank said, pushing David away. "We haven't had breakfast and I'm starving."

"Later," David said under his breath. "Remember the—"

The man placed his hand on David's shoulder. "Can't argue with an empty stomach," he said. "Besides you haven't answered my question. Where are your folks?"

"Gone."

"Not here."

"Dead," said Frank.

Kathy gasped at the use of the word.

Frank looked at her shocked face and shrugged. "Well, they're not alive right now, are they?"

That was true, if the newspaper was right. But "not born yet" sounded a lot better than "dead." An uncomfortable feeling settled around Kathy. A whisper tickled at the back of her mind. "To save this man you may be late, but more's at stake than one man's fate." She rubbed her temple and frowned. Was someone's life in danger?

"If you have no parents, who's taking care of you?" the stranger asked. "Where are you staying?"

David crossed his arms and stood straight and tall, matching the man in height. "We take care of ourselves."

"Yes, I can see that," the man said dryly, glancing at Kathy's manure-spattered clothes and the dirt stains on David's and Frank's jeans. His mustache twitched as he tried to hide a smile. "But tell me," he said, "do you have money for food or lodging?"

The three looked blankly at each other. Frank dug his hand into his back pocket and pulled out a small red pocketknife and a book of matches. He stared at the items, then snorted. He shoved them back into his pocket, not bothering to check his windbreaker. Kathy patted her own denim jacket and jeans to no avail, while David raised a shiny quarter in triumph. When Frank mouthed "wrong date," he quickly slipped it out of sight.

"As I thought," the stranger said, eyeing the trio up and down. His gaze paused again on the nylon jackets and tennis shoes. "I've got a few extra coins today," he finally said. "I reckon I can buy you breakfast. I wouldn't mind a cup of coffee myself." He grinned and held out his hand. "I'm Joe Sturtevant, but most folks call me Rocky Mountain Joe."

Frank seized his hand and pumped it up and down. "Frank Kessler," he said, "and this is David and Kathy."

David shook Joe's hand once, then quickly pulled away. To Kathy, Joe bowed low and winked. She couldn't help but smile.

"We'll go to the Belvidere," he said, straightening up. "It's a decent hotel and George is a generous man. He'll feed you up right. Then, we'll talk."

He led them down the street, stopping briefly to chat with some men along the way. David pulled Frank and Kathy aside.

"What are we going to tell him?" he asked, dropping his voice to a hush.

64

"We're orphans," Frank replied with a shrug. "I told him our parents were dead."

"But how do we explain our clothes? He keeps staring at our jackets and I don't think nylon's been invented yet." David frowned and leaned closer to his sister and Frank. "I think he's the one," he said. "He's the only one who's smiled all day. I don't think we should tell him anything."

"We've got to eat," Frank said, not bothering to keep his voice down. "Besides, it can't be him. He lives here. Whoever we're looking for goes up Boulder Canyon. That's what *my* riddle says."

Kathy rubbed at a growing pressure in her head, trying to push away the ache. None of this made sense. She couldn't recall Frank's riddle. She only remembered parts of David's because he kept repeating it. "What if he's not the one?" she asked. "He seems awfully nice."

"He smiled, didn't he?" David growled.

Kathy couldn't argue with that, but somehow that didn't seem enough. Frowning, she massaged her forehead. Maybe she was just hungry.

Joe finished his conversation and beckoned for the trio to join him. Waving to people along the way, he guided them through town until they came to a two-story wooden building with a long bench propped along the front. Several men sat outside chatting or chewing tobacco while others leaned against the wall, half-asleep.

"Here we are," he said, opening the door and gesturing for Kathy to walk through first. He ushered them into the dining area and directed them to an empty table. "George," he called to a man who hurried to greet them. "I've brought you some customers."

George squinted at the children and frowned, especially at Kathy in her jeans. "They're not the rascals who've been rigging tripwires all over town, are they?"

Joe's lips twitched with amusement as he eyed Frank and David. "I haven't had time to ask. Are you?"

"Are we what?" David responded, his voice loud and defensive.

"Are you the scamps who've been stringing wire across the boardwalks, tripping decent folk?"

David shook his head in indignation. "No way, we just got here. Besides, Mom and Dad would kill us." He slapped his hand over his mouth at his mistake, then quickly dropped it to his side as he assumed a blank face.

Frank barely stifled a giggle. He leaned over to Kathy and whispered, "Not a bad idea." She pushed him away in disgust.

Joe watched the interchange, then turned to George. "I don't think they're the culprits, but I do believe they're hungry. How about some pancakes for the rascals and coffee for me?"

George grunted and hurried out the door.

True to his reputation, George served generous stacks

of pancakes, dripping with gooey molasses. Beside each plate he placed a glass of cold milk. Kathy chewed slowly, savoring every sticky bite, while David and Frank shoveled the food into their mouths as fast as the flapjacks were plopped on their plates. Rocky Mountain Joe sat quietly, sipping a cup of coffee.

"You three ever been to a circus?" he asked after David and Frank had finished their second round of pancakes and were starting on their third.

All three of them glanced at each other, then slowly shook their heads.

"No?" Joe said, watching them closely. "When I was a lad, I was apprenticed as a broom-maker to a hardworking man. It was a good profession. I would have done well. But the circus came to town and lured me with its glamour. So off I went. I met some folks with the oddest clothes and shoes," he said, raising an eyebrow at the trio. "I stayed with them until the war broke out. Then I joined the army."

"What war?" Frank mumbled through a mouthful of food.

"Which war," Joe corrected him. "I fought in two: the War of Southern Aggression and the Indian Wars."

"You fought in the Civil War?" David asked.

"You fought Indians?" Frank chimed in, his voice drowning out David's.

Rocky Mountain Joe nodded. "I was captured twice. First time, another man and I were tied to the ground. Our captors planned to burn us. Then a storm blew up, pouring rain. While we were left alone, we pulled those stakes up out of the soggy soil and hightailed it out of there. The second time, Chief Sitting Bull kept me prisoner for two years. I escaped by floating down the Missouri River."

Frank was silent for only a second or two before bursting out a flood of questions, each one launching Joe on another story about his life as an Indian scout and fighter. Every now and then, David squeaked in a question about the Civil War or the circus.

Kathy barely listened. The pressure in her head still pushed forward, nagging at her. She ran her fork across her plate to smooth the leftover molasses into a silky sheen. With the tip of her fork she began to doodle, etching out the lines of a large old tree with drooping branches. Halfway through a story, Joe reached over, took the fork from her fingers, and added a small bird on the lowermost branch.

"Can't have a tree without a blackbird," he said with a smile. He laid the fork down and leaned back in his chair. "Now, I want to hear about you."

"We're orphans," Kathy said, not daring to meet his eyes. "We're looking for someone and we're not sure how to find him."

David kicked her under the table and gave her an exasperated glare. "Our uncle," he said quickly. "We're looking for our uncle."

"Has he got a name?" Joe asked

David stammered, a panicked look on his face, but nothing intelligible came out.

"Tree," Frank muttered under his breath as he stared at Kathy's plate. "Tree—oak—staff." He looked up and said, "Staff. Robert Staff. We're looking for our Uncle Bob."

David gave Frank a grateful look. "That's right," he said. "We're looking for our uncle, but we've never met him."

"You're brothers and sister, then?" Joe asked, cocking an eye at Frank.

"Not him," Kathy blurted. Frank glowered at her while David kicked her from under the table again.

"We're cousins," David said, giving Kathy a look that told her to be quiet.

"And *all* your parents are dead?" Joe asked.

"It's like this," Frank said slowly, as he stared at the crumbs on his plate. "We're cousins. Grew up near each other, but there was—an epidemic, cholera or something, and our parents died. So we decided to look for Uncle Bob. It's just—we're not sure where to find him except—he might be heading up Boulder Canyon."

Rocky Mountain Joe sat quiet and still, sharp eyes boring into each of them. Kathy squirmed in her seat and was just about to burst when he laughed.

"I do love a good tale. And your clothes? What is your story for that?"

No one answered.

"Never mind," he said. "I'll leave it to my imagination. Still, you need money and a place to stay, and I do believe you are looking for *someone*. I think I can help. The best place to look for a traveling man is at the hotels. If your 'uncle' is heading up the canyon, the Brainard Hotel is a good bet. The Caribou Stage has an office there and Annie Brainard could use extra help right now—serving guests and cleaning rooms. Kathy could help Annie out, have a few good meals, and earn a little money." He eyed her jeans and denim jacket. "You'll need some proper clothes, though. The church has been running a charity drive. I bet they'll have something fit for you to wear."

Frank snickered under his breath. "Waiting tables and cleaning rooms. This should be good."

"You'll have to work, too, if you want to eat," Joe said. "You might help out at a stable. There's one across the street from the Brainard, but if you want to cover more territory, the Stone Barn would be best. In fact, yesterday Simpson mentioned he could use some help."

Frank sat up straight. "Stables? I get to work with horses?"

"Maybe," Joe replied.

"Yes!" Frank hissed under his breath.

David cleared his throat. "One of us should walk around town to check out the other places."

Joe nodded, then pointed to Frank's and David's clothing. "You could use some boots and coats, too, if the church has them. Otherwise," he said with an odd smile, "folks might think you've run away from the circus." He pushed himself up from the table. "It's best we get started."

David rose from his chair, his brow furrowed in thought. "Are the stagecoaches the only way to go up the canyon?" he asked.

"Not at all," Joe replied, after taking one last sip of his coffee. "Some folks rent horses, other folks walk. Tomorrow, I'm catching a ride up on a wagon, myself."

David and Frank both stopped dead in their tracks.

"You're going up Boulder Canyon?" Frank asked, his voice barely above a squeak.

"Sure am," Joe replied.

7 The Map

Why did Joe have to go up Boulder Canyon? Why couldn't he just stay put? With an irritated *snap,* Kathy flipped the last clean, wet sheet onto the clothesline, then wrinkled her nose at the nearby three-hole outhouse marked LADIES on one side and MEN on the other. The outhouse for the two-storied Brainard Hotel smelled as sour as her day had gone ever since Joe had mentioned his pending trip.

David and Frank had whispered together after their pancake brunch, each with an ominous look on his face.

Kathy had tried to join them, to argue it couldn't be Joe, but oddly Joe kept getting in the way. It was the darn clothes. The darn shoes. Why did girls *have* to wear dresses?

Walking beside Kathy, Joe had led them to the church where a bevy of ladies sequestered her in a private room and bundled her up in layer after layer of clothes: shoes, socks, underdrawers, petticoat, chemise, dress, and apron. The boys, on the other hand, only had to try on a few worn boots and a tattered coat or two.

Next they went to the hotel, where Mrs. Brainard, in her relief, had hustled Kathy into the building so quickly there had been barely enough time to wave goodbye to David and Frank. Kathy knew by the looks on the boys' faces they were convinced Joe was the black-hearted man in the riddle. After hours of hard labor, Kathy was beginning to wonder if they were right.

Holding her nose, she grabbed the empty basket and hobbled toward the kitchen door. The black high-topped shoes rummaged from the church rubbed blisters on her feet and chafed her ankles where rows of buttons ran up their sides. The tiny beads tightened the leather against coarse wool stockings. She didn't know what was worse, the blisters or the itching.

Mrs. Brainard glanced at her as she entered the kitchen. "Kathy, the customer in Room Five left for the day—finally. Such a difficult man! Could you run upstairs and clean the room for me, dear? I don't know when he'll be back."

Kathy slowly climbed the stairs, her tired legs and sore feet protesting each step. She tapped on the guest room door and waited a minute, just in case the man had returned. Then she pushed it open.

The quilted bedcover and blankets lay crumpled on the floor. Wadded-up paper and bits of trash littered the carpet. Water dripped off the marble top of the washstand, where it had spilled out of the washbowl, and newspaper clippings and papers threatened to tumble off the corner desk.

"What a slob," Kathy grumbled, scratching her arms under the faded, gray-blue wool dress the church ladies had given her. Moving with care, she gathered up paper and trash from the floor and stuffed the refuse into the small potbellied stove used for heating the room, all except the broken pencil found under the washstand. Thinking she might need it, she slipped the splintered stub into the pocket of the work apron covering her dress.

She emptied the washbowl and the water pitcher out the window, after checking to make sure no one was below. She made the bed and tucked in the covers. Then, with a rustling of papers, she straightened the mess on the desk.

Newspaper clippings featuring reports on gold and silver mines littered the wooden surface. Most had peculiar names: the Horsfal, the Smuggler, the Wamego, the Golden Age. Kathy fingered the articles, wondering if they were important. Didn't the riddle say something about gold, something more than just the golden smile?

Or did it? She groaned in frustration. Why couldn't she remember?

She stacked the clippings together into a pile, along with stagecoach and train schedules. Everything seemed to be about money and where to find it.

Kathy looked around the clean room and grimaced at the one last task that remained. Wrinkling her nose, she bent down, pulled out the lidded pot from under the bed, and opened it. It was empty. Relieved, she pushed the chamber pot back, took one last look at the newspaper articles, then left.

She had just reached the bottom of the stairs when Mrs. Brainard rushed by, scurrying to the kitchen.

"Kathy, I need your help. Folks are arriving for supper."

So soon? Kathy thought as she poked her head around the dining room door to see who was there. Already several groups of people had settled into chairs around the cloth-covered tables. Kathy sighed. It would be a long night.

"Take orders for me, dear," Mrs. Brainard said as she joined Kathy at the doorway. The landlady smoothed her hair and her black sateen dress with her hands, then rustled into the room to greet her guests.

Following her employer's example, Kathy straightened her apron and tucked stray strands of hair behind her ears. Scanning the room for a friendly face, she walked over to a table where a woman sat with her two boys and little girl. A dusty smell combined with sweat suggested they had just arrived in town. The little girl, no more than four, stretched her neck to see over the tablecloth. Thumping short legs on her chair, she gazed at Kathy with emerald-green eyes.

"May I help you?" Kathy asked.

"Aye, please." The woman replied in an odd, lilting accent. She smiled despite the strain that showed on her face. "We're some hungry, aren't we, me dears?" The two boys nodded enthusiastically, while the little girl continued to stare. The gaze felt uncomfortable, and, oddly, familiar.

Kathy looked away. She cleared her throat and scanned her memory for what the cook was preparing. "Tonight we have roast chicken and pot roast with gravy, boiled or mashed potatoes, boiled carrots, and stewed green peas," she said, mentally walking herself through the kitchen. "Pickles, sliced tomatoes, and cheese." She winked at the boys, whose eyes had grown round as little moons. "For dessert there's green apple pie and sponge cake with raspberries. We also have coffee, tea, and cold milk. Oh, and biscuits." Kathy's mouth watered at the thought of the white, fluffy biscuits served at lunch with hot, melting butter oozing down their sides. She had saved all the untouched ones abandoned on customers' plates and stashed them in a small box in the hallway closet, close (but not too close) to her T-shirt, jacket, and soiled jeans. She hadn't forgotten her hunger from that morning, and the biscuits were so good.

The little girl tapped her mother's arm. "Can I have a biscuit?" she asked.

The woman laughed and stroked her daughter's dark brown hair. "Aas, Emily love, as long as you stay well." She turned to Kathy. "We left Caribou this morning because of the diphtheria. Matthew, my husband, wants to keep the children safe."

Kathy smiled, not knowing what to say. She'd never heard of diphtheria and didn't know what it was. But now wasn't a good time to ask.

Soon the clatter of forks and knives rang through the dining room as more people filed in. Kathy hurried back and forth between the tables and the kitchen, taking orders and serving food. She tried hard not to limp.

Most of the customers were men. Some whispered excitedly about a promising gold or silver strike, while others gravely discussed how this mine or that wasn't producing well and might soon shut down. Still others talked about business deals, this year's crops, the railroad, or how dry the summer had been. Almost all were well dressed. The Brainard was one of the best hotels in town.

Every time someone said "gold," Kathy's ears perked up, but no one looked like a gold miner to her. What was it the riddle had said, anyway?

A man in a long, crisp coat with a tidy white handkerchief tucked in his breast pocket rapped the top of his table with the ivory handle of his walking stick. He had the air of a wealthy man. "Little lady?" he called, stroking his mutton-chop sideburns. "We could use more coffee."

Kathy grabbed a pot of hot brew from the kitchen and hurried back, giving a wide berth to the adjacent table, occupied by a surly man with a greasy mustache. He had eaten very little, but watched everyone in the dining room with squinty eyes that reminded Kathy of her uncle's cat, Diablo, just before he pounced on a bird. A receding hairline and pencil-thin eyebrows even made his forehead bulge like the cat's. She could almost see the man's tail flicking.

She poured steaming coffee into the rich man's cup and offered some to his companion, a scruffy man with a worn, crumpled coat and ratty beard. The second man shook his head, looking ill at ease and out of place in the Brainard. The gentleman sipped his coffee. "You've done a lot of mining," he said to his companion. "I take it you know your ores, and you know how to read a good map. So what is this about a gold mine?"

Kathy nearly dropped the coffeepot. A map? Didn't David's riddle say something about a map? Why couldn't she remember, when her own riddle was so clear?

She wanted to stay and listen, but the surly cat-man raised his empty cup and snapped his fingers for more coffee. Annoyed, Kathy hurried to his side, nearly spilling the coffee in her agitation. As if amused, the man curled his lip into a half-smile. His greasy, unkempt mustache curled around his mouth and plastered itself against the man's upper teeth, hiding all but the tiniest glimmer of dull yellow. Above the mustache, long black hairs stuck out of his nostrils, like coarse bristles on a brush. Kathy's own lips twitched in revulsion. She struggled not to stare. Nose clippers, she thought. Somebody should buy the man nose clippers.

Forcing herself to look away, she splashed coffee into the nose-man's cup, then edged back toward the map conversation. Spying an empty table nearby, she put down the coffee, grabbed a cloth napkin, and dusted the centerpiece—blossoms, vase, and all. Leaning toward the two men, she strained to eavesdrop.

The scruffy miner scratched his beard, dirt showing under his ragged fingernails. "You see, my friend visited Centennial Ridge in Wyoming last year. The Centennial Lode is a rich one, but darn if the vein don't stop dead in the mountain. Some fault just cut that vein in two and moved the other half somewhere else. Nobody's been able to figure out where. Nobody, that is, but my friend." The miner sat back in his chair and smiled, thumbs sticking in his vest pockets.

"And?" the gentleman asked.

The miner leaned forward and whispered, "I've got his map and I'm looking for investors." He reached into his inside coat pocket and pulled out a folded piece of paper. Carefully straightening it out, he placed the paper in the middle of the table. Kathy edged closer, pulling the vase of flowers with her.

"Miss," a man called from across the room. "I'd like another piece of pie."

Kathy glared. She plopped the rumpled napkin next to the coffee pot and hurried into the kitchen. She nearly dropped the pie on the man's lap as she rushed back. She grabbed the napkin again and began to dust the chairs, hoping she hadn't missed anything important.

The gentleman tossed the map into the center of the table. "What kind of directions are these—a thousand feet by blackbird's wings, four hundred feet by nightly owl? This map doesn't show anything except the original lode and that location isn't any secret. And what's this funny-looking mark down here?"

The miner quickly shook his head. "No, you don't understand. Like I told you, my friend has the mark of the tommyknockers. It's the missing piece."

"What good is a map if it's not all there?" the rich man scoffed. "And all this superstitious talk. What do you take me for, a fool?" He pushed back his chair, reached into the pocket of his trousers, and pulled out a one-dollar coin. "Young lady," he called. "I need some change."

Kathy almost dropped the coin as she strained to get a good look at the map, but the miner quickly picked it up, folded it, and put it back inside his coat.

"Sir," he said, "I can assure you I am not making this up. My friend has the sight. Ask his boss in Caribou. He knows where the veins go and when they're running out. The knockers tell him."

"Pshh," the wealthy man replied. "I'm not going to invest money on a fool's lark. You haven't even filed a claim!"

"That's just the point. We've got to hurry before someone else finds the lode."

The wealthy man dismissed his companion with a wave of his hand and placed his derby hat on his head. "I need my change," he said crossly to Kathy.

"Yes, sir," Kathy replied. Sore feet and tired legs forgotten, she trotted as fast as her narrow skirt would allow to the parlor, where the clerk received guests and handled the money. She waited impatiently as the clerk counted out the change, and nearly snatched it from his hand. But apparently she was too late. The gentleman stormed through the parlor and out the front door, leaving his money behind. Stunned, Kathy stared after him. Fearful that the miner might be right behind, she hurried back to the dining room. He still sat at the table, shaking his head and mumbling.

"I shouldn't tell them about the knockers. Scares them every time." He looked up, startled, to see Kathy standing there. "I'm afraid my companion left and I best be leaving, too." He dug into his pants pocket, pulling out several coins. "Here's for the meal and a little extra for you."

"Thanks," Kathy said. She slipped the extra coin into

her apron pocket along with the other man's change.

The miner rose and walked toward the parlor, his heavy boots clumping on the floor. Frantically, Kathy looked around. How was she going to keep track of him when there were customers left? She couldn't just leave. But he had a map. Maybe he stole it! Maybe *he* was the bad guy! Maybe Joe was all right.

Still struggling about what to do, Kathy started after the miner. She was halfway to the parlor when the nose-hair man stood up, knocking back his chair. "Girl! I need change. Quick now!" He flipped a coin in her direction. She missed the catch. Dropping to her knees, she scrambled after the money, hoping she still had time to follow the map man.

"Forget it," the nose-hair man snapped. "Keep the change." He strode toward the parlor door and nearly collided with David, who was just entering the room. The man thrust Kathy's brother against the door frame, pushing him out of the way. David tried to protest, but the man never slowed down.

Ignoring the stray coin, Kathy ran over to David, nearly tripping in her dress. "David," she said, snatching his arm, "I think I found the map. Didn't your riddle say something about a map? And the bad guy, I think I found him, too. Quick, you've got to follow him."

"Wh—what?" David said, still flustered from being manhandled. "But I thought Joe—"

"A scruffy guy, he just left, he has a map, a gold mine map. Quick, don't let him get away."

"What? Wait! I'm hungry!"

"No time, go!" She shoved her brother into the parlor and out the front door. She pointed after the miner who was crossing the street almost a block away. "Run."

David took one look at his sister's face, then darted down the street.

Kathy watched him go, her heart pounding in her chest. Oh please, oh please, oh please, she prayed. Let that be the man—not Joe. Not nice Joe Sturtevant. Turning away, she limped back to the dining room and looked at the now empty tables. Neither the wealthy man nor the miner had eaten much. Their plates were still full of roast chicken, boiled potatoes, and peas. They hadn't touched the biscuits, either. Kathy smiled. David and Frank would eat well tonight, and there was still that coin on the floor. Figuring the coin could wait, she picked up the plates and headed for the kitchen.

8 The Stone Barn

What did you find out?" Kathy asked her brother, as she watched David and Frank gobble the food she had salvaged from the hotel. She had wanted to bring more, but the kitchen had been surprisingly bare after serving so many dinner guests, and each time Kathy squirreled away a biscuit or a piece of cheese, Mrs. Brainard gave her an odd look. It wasn't until Kathy had finished her chores and left the hotel to join David and Frank at the Stone Barn that she discovered a small jug of milk tucked inside her box, along with several pieces of pie, carefully wrapped in brown paper. The pie was the first thing to disappear into the boys' hungry mouths.

"Well?" she added, kicking her heels impatiently against the bale of hay that served as a chair. Dried bits of grass pricked her legs, tickling skin that already itched from the coarse wool fabric of her socks and dress. She reached down and scratched.

David waved at her to be patient, then chugged cold

milk to wash down the biscuit he had been chewing. "I followed that guy to George's place," he said, wiping bits of cream off his upper lip with his sleeve. "He's renting a room upstairs. Did you know a room only costs twenty-five cents? That's all a meal costs, too. I found a quarter between the boardwalk slats and had lunch."

"What?" Frank mumbled through a mouthful of chicken. "You had lunch and didn't bring *me* any? I haven't eaten since breakfast."

Kathy could believe it. Frank had wolfed down two pieces of chicken, three bites of cheese, two biscuits, and one piece of pie in the last fifteen minutes. She had never seen anyone eat so fast, and with just one hand. His other hand had kept busy swatting at black flies that hovered near his food. Flies seemed to buzz everywhere in the dim light of the livery stable, the whine of their wings mingling with the soft rustle of horses and mules.

"It was only beef stew," David said. "I had no way to carry it. Besides, I thought the stable guys would feed you."

"Well, you thought wrong," Frank said. With a snort, he reached for a biscuit from David's pile of food and stuck it on top of his own. David started to protest, but then changed his mind and shrugged. "That's fair."

Kathy didn't think so. She had taken great pains to divvy the smuggled food from the Brainard into two equal parts. Then she remembered the sugar-cured ham, boiled potatoes, tomatoes, pickled beets, cheese, and cole slaw served for lunch that day—not to mention the custard pie with the huge drops of gold beading on top. She was only given leftover trimmings to eat, but they still had been a feast.

"David," she said, poking him with a finger. "What about the man?"

"Him? Oh, he stayed in his room for a while, and then came here. He must board a horse or something, because he talked to some guy, went inside for a while, and then came out."

Frank coughed, nearly choking on his food. "You mean he was right here? I didn't see him. Are you sure?"

"Yeah, I'm sure," David replied, sounding testy.

"You wouldn't know him, anyway," Kathy said, tugging at her narrow skirt. She pushed and pulled her legs in an effort to sit cross-legged, but the petticoat and dress held tight. With a grunt, she gave up and leaned over to massage her tender foot through the stiff black leather shoe. "You don't know what he looks like," she wheezed from her awkward position. "And he's kind of hard to describe." She grimaced at the sting from her blisters, but she didn't dare take off her shoes. It had taken a wire hook to button them up at the church. She couldn't do it with just her fingers. Without the help of the wire gadget, she'd have to wear her tennis shoes. They'd be more comfortable, but probably everyone in town would notice and shower her with scowls and frowns.

"It doesn't matter, anyway," David said, looking sideways at Kathy. "I don't think he's the guy. I think it's Rocky Mountain Joe. He's the only person who smiled today and he *is* going up Boulder Canyon."

"But what about the map?" Kathy protested. "Didn't your riddle say something about a map?" Despite the day's frustrations, she couldn't believe Joe was bad.

"Yeah," David said slowly, "but the riddle mentioned the smile first. Did you ever see the man with the map smile?'

Kathy had to admit she hadn't. The man had looked uncomfortable and nervous the whole time he was at the Brainard.

Frank swallowed and took a swig of water. "I think it's Joe, too," he said. "I can't remember the other riddles, so I've been thinking about mine. It definitely says this guy we're looking for goes up Boulder Canyon to . . . what did it say? . . . 'pursue his own gold lust?' Maybe it's talking about a gold mine, but certainly not one in Wyoming. I don't think you found the right map." He flicked loose straw in Kathy's direction. "The problem is there are hundreds of mines in the mountains west of here. Thousands maybe. How are we ever going to know which one?"

Scowling, Kathy brushed away the straw that had fallen on her dress. Frank had a point but she didn't want to admit it and she still didn't think Joe was the man.

"I saw the names of a bunch of mines today in one of the guest rooms," she offered, ignoring the snicker from Frank as several pieces of straw snagged on the wool of her skirt. "They had some really strange names. One was the Golden Age. Maybe there's one called the Golden Smile. Maybe that's what the riddle means—the man who owns the Golden Smile mine. It could be the man from supper."

"I don't know," David said, shaking his head. "That would be a weird name for a mine, don't you think?"

"No weirder than the others," Kathy replied flicking straw back at Frank. "And it *is* a map. Your riddle said something about a map, right? And it's a map to a gold mine, too."

"Well, I'm not going to worry about it tonight," Frank said, crumpling up the brown paper that had held the pie and tossing it to the ground. "I am so tired I can hardly think. Besides, it's not so bad being here. I mean, I got to work with the horses and mules, brush them down, feed them, pick their feet. I never get to do anything like that at home and—well, it's history. It's living, breathing history. It's much better than reading a book. Maybe we should stay a while."

"No!" Kathy said with alarm. A sharp pain pressed against her forehead. "We can't! We've got to solve the riddle. We've got to hurry because—because. I don't know why, but I know we do. My riddle says something about being late. 'To save this man you may be late.' We can't be late. What if someone dies?"

She looked at her brother, hoping to find support, but he seemed confused as he glanced back and forth between his sister and Frank. Kathy turned back toward Frank, her eyes pleading for him to understand, hoping that for once he would be nice.

Frank returned her gaze as if trying to read her mind. He didn't snicker and he didn't smirk. Instead, his face was somber.

"You're right," he finally said, dropping his eyes and poking the straw bale with his finger. "It's just . . . I can't remember your riddle, that's all."

"Me, neither," David said with a scowl on his face. "I don't know why. It can't be *that* hard."

Kathy frowned. David could memorize just about anything, including the name of every soccer player who played in last year's World Cup. Why couldn't he memorize now? She kicked the bale of hay beneath her and dug her hands deep into her apron pocket. Her fingers pressed against something hard. Suddenly she smiled. "Let's write it down," she said, pulling out the broken pencil she had found that day. She picked up the discarded wrapping paper and tore off the parts sticky with pie. Straightening what was left, she wrote *Riddle* at the top.

"Okay, David," she said. "You start."

David nodded and began to recite. Syllable after syllable tumbled off the tip of his tongue, but Kathy couldn't understand a word. "Stop horsing around, David," she said. "This is serious."

"I'm not horsing around," he replied. He glanced at the nearly blank paper on Kathy's lap. "Why aren't you writing?"

"What do you think?" Kathy answered, glaring at her brother. "Because you're talking garbage. That's why."

"Sounded okay to me," Frank said with a shrug. "Maybe you're just tired. Here, let me write." He tugged the brown paper and the pencil from Kathy's resistant hands, then settled the crinkled sheet on his knees. "Okay," he said, grinning at David. "I'm ready."

Again David recited his riddle. This time it made sense to Kathy, but Frank just sat there, a confused look on his face. "Knock it off," he said. "Now you *are* talking gibberish. It's not funny."

"Oh, stop it," Kathy said, turning her frustration toward Frank. "He said everything right."

"No, he didn't," Frank snapped back. "He was talking . . . well, I don't know what he was talking, but nothing made sense."

"Right," David said, rolling his eyes. "Here, give it to me. I'll write it." He snatched the pencil and paper from Frank and pressed the leaded point down. But he didn't write. His hand sat unmoving on the ragged page.

"Well?" Kathy said.

David looked up, alarmed. "I can't remember it. I just had it, but now. . . ." He took a deep breath and closed his eyes. His lips moved as he quietly recited his verse to himself. Feeling for the paper, he pressed the pencil down to write, but then everything stopped: the pencil, his hand, his lips. David sat there, mouth hanging open as if waiting for words to come. Finally he snapped his jaw shut and opened his eyes. "I'm too tired to think anyway," he growled. With an irritated wave of his hand, he brushed the paper and pencil to the ground. "Let's just go to bed. We can worry about the riddle tomorrow."

Kathy watched the pencil tumble and come to rest in the straw. She was tired, too: tired from lack of sleep; tired from hours of washing sheets, cleaning rooms, and serving meals; tired from thinking about a riddle she could only partially remember. Somehow, she knew the riddle would never get written down, no matter how much they tried.

With a sigh, she brushed several strands of hair away from her face. At least they had beds, sort of. Frank had talked the stable owner into letting them spend the night in the barn, assuring the man that they would keep an eye on the horses. A bed at the Brainard would have been nicer. Kathy hadn't thought to ask.

With arms heavy and sore from the day's work, she pushed herself off the straw bale, then picked up the pencil and slipped it back into her apron pocket. She reached for the ladder. Careful of the blisters on her feet, she slowly climbed the steps and pulled herself up over the top and onto the wooden loft. The light was dim, just a soft wash that rippled up over the edge of the loft or trickled through cracks in the floor. Kathy hesitated a moment, then grabbed one of the blankets the stable owner had loaned them and hobbled to the far corner, where she had stashed her clothes and the box filled with salvaged potatoes, biscuits, and cheese. She sniffed toward the clothes and grunted with satisfaction. Her jeans and shoes didn't smell so bad now that the manure had dried and been mostly brushed off. But then, she was in a barn and the whole place smelled slightly of manure. Oddly, Kathy didn't mind.

Shaking the blanket out, she folded it neatly into a cocoon on the straw-littered floor next to her pile of clothes. She had just flipped back the top to crawl in when Frank's head popped over the top of the ladder.

"You going to bed in your shoes?"

"I don't dare take them off," she replied. "I can't button them back up without some hook thing."

"What kind of hook thing?" he asked as he grabbed a blanket and walked over to her side.

"I can't describe it very well," she said, "but it fastens these little buttons."

Frank bent over and peered at the black shiny knobs in the dim light, then felt them with his fingers. With a snort, he straightened up, fished into his pocket, and

93

pulled out his red pocketknife. He flipped open one of the blades, revealing a can opener with a small hook on the inside.

"Ta-da!" he said. "This will button them up. Promise."

Kathy grinned and quickly unhooked the high-topped shoes. She tugged them off and flung them into a darkened corner. Her feet felt so much better.

"Thanks," she said.

"Welcome," Frank replied with a grin. He picked up his blanket and walked over to the other corner, where David was burrowing in the hay. Kathy crawled between the folds of her blanket and pulled it snug around her to ward off the cool night air. For once she was grateful for all her layers of clothing. She wouldn't be cold tonight.

From the far corner, she could hear Frank mutter, then shuffle his way to the ladder and down. The night

filled with inky darkness as he turned out the kerosene lamps. Clatters, clanks, and creaks followed him back as he felt his way up the ladder and over to the far corner of the loft where David's exhausted snores thrummed loudly.

"Be quiet," Frank's voice complained in the darkness. A thud and rustle suggested he had tried to wake David. Kathy smiled. Frank was in for a long night.

She lay awake staring into the darkness as sounds settled around her: the scritch-scratch of mice in the straw, the harrumphs of horses and mules, a creak here, a shuffle there. Unlike household creaks, the sounds of the stable floated gently over her, lulling her to sleep. Somehow she didn't think there would be whispers here.

As her mind faded into a snowy haze, a barn owl hooted in the night. *Who who, who who.* The sound drifted in the air, weaving in and out among the snorts and snuffles. It murmured in her ear, joined by a flapping of feathers as a cool night breeze fluttered over her face. Wings spread wide and lifted her up, floating toward a flickering light and whispering voices.

Whispering voices!

Kathy woke with a start.

She held her breath, trying to listen over the pounding of her heart. Footsteps thumped on hardened dirt below, followed by the murmur of a deep voice and an answering nicker.

Somebody was downstairs.

9 Fire!

"Frank!" Kathy hissed into the darkness.

She eased out from under the blanket and, on hands and knees, crept toward the other corner of the loft. "Frank!" she hissed again, wishing David wasn't such a heavy sleeper.

"What?" a sleepy voice grumbled. The straw in the corner rustled as a dark silhouette rose against the flickering light reflected off the ceiling beams. "What do you want?"

"Somebody's downstairs."

Frank rubbed his eyes, then tossed his blanket on David and crawled over to the edge of the loft. Gripping the wooden side, he stretched out into the air and bent over to get a look. Kathy leaned over the rim beside him. Below, in the pale glow of a kerosene lamp, a man stood by a closed stall door, stroking the nose of a dapple-gray horse.

"Is he supposed to be there?" Kathy whispered.

"I don't know," Frank replied. "I better go check. I'm supposed to guard the barn."

Bent low, he tiptoed back to the corner, pulled on his boots, then headed for the ladder. Careful not to make any sound, he grabbed the top and swung himself around. As Frank clambered down, Kathy bent over to get a better view. She almost leaned too far. She wobbled and began to lose her balance when a hand reached around and pulled her back.

"What are you, nuts?" David said in her ear.

Kathy turned, surprised to see him awake. "Shh," she said and pointed below.

Frank stepped off the last rung, then hesitated at the foot of the ladder. Rubbing his hands together, he contemplated the man. After a moment, he took a deep breath, straightened his shoulders, and strode toward the stranger.

"Can I help you?" he asked.

"No, thank you," the man replied, caressing the horse's forehead. "I'm just checking on my horse before I call it a night. I'm rather fond of him, you see."

"He's a nice animal," Frank said, stepping beside the man to rub the dapple-gray nose. "I fed and watered him myself."

"Much obliged," the stranger said, turning toward Frank and into the light. Kathy clutched her brother's arm. "David," she said, "that's the map man! We've got to warn Frank. He doesn't know what he looks like." She twisted around toward the ladder and pushed herself up. Her brother grabbed her arm and held her back.

"Wait," he said.

Giving in to her brother's pull, she crouched down and watched while Frank and the stranger chatted. She wondered if the man had the map now, hidden in his pocket. She wondered if his heart was really black. Minutes ticked by as Kathy's muscles tightened into uncomfortable knots and a mustiness filled the air. Below, the horses and mules shuffled uneasily in their stalls. Kathy wrinkled her nose and fought the urge to sneeze, until the musty odor shifted into a whiff of smoke.

"Frank!" she cried, causing Frank and the man below to jump. "Something's burning!"

Frank looked around, confused. "I don't smell anything."

Two horses stamped on the ground in agitation. Others paced back and forth in their pens.

David sat up and sniffed. "I don't smell it, either," he said, an odd frown on his face, "but I think I hear it. Frank, something's burning."

In an unused stall near the stable exit, a faint crackle popped in the air as tiny tongues of flame flickered through the wooden slats.

"Fire!" the map man shouted, running over to the stall. "Bring water, quick." He stomped on the fire with his heavy boots even as it reached the wooden railing. Dark tendrils of smoke curled into the air, filled with ammonia from damp, urine-soaked hay. All around the barn, horses neighed in alarm, tossing their heads and slashing their hooves against the wooden boards that confined them. Loud frantic brays added to the uproar.

Frank grabbed the nearest watering bucket and raced to the stall, spilling precious fluid on the ground. The map man snatched the bucket from Frank's hands and tossed the water on the growing flames that licked the wooden railing. "Get the animals out!" he yelled. "Sound the alarm."

Not waiting to put on shoes, Kathy and David scrambled down the ladder. David pushed Kathy toward the door. "Get help," he hollered through the din of frightened animals. "And stay out of the barn!" He snatched a shovel from a pile of tools nearby and ran to join the miner.

Kathy dashed outside and twirled around, confused. She didn't know which way to run.

"Fire," she screamed at the top of her voice. "Fire! Somebody help!"

A light flickered on at a building down the street and a man stepped out onto the boardwalk. He glanced at the barn and Kathy's frantic gesturing, then ran down the street in the opposite direction, shouting as he went. Kathy stared after him, wondering what to do now.

"Help!" Frank called to her as he struggled to lead the dapple-gray horse past the burning stall and out of the barn. It tossed its head, rearing back, eyes rolling white with fear.

100

Kathy ran toward Frank and the frantic horse. She tried to grab the horse's head, but seemed only to get in Frank's way. Then she remembered a story sitting on her bookshelf. Dodging past the struggling pair, Kathy dashed into the barn and snatched a blanket from a nearby rail. "Throw this on its head," she hollered, trying to be heard over the screams and brays of the terrified horses and mules.

Frank grabbed the blanket and flung it at the horse's head. The cloth fell haphazardly over its face, covering its eyes. Blinded by the blanket, the horse froze long enough for Frank to grab its halter, pull its head down, and lead it outside. He pulled the blanket off and released the animal into the night.

"Come on," he shouted. "We've got to get the others out." Together, they ran inside the barn, past the miner and David, who fought the fire with water, dirt, and a smoldering blanket. Through the thick, stinging smoke, Kathy couldn't tell if they were winning. She and Frank had led three more horses outside when an arm reached over and yanked her shoulder.

"I told you to stay outside," David yelled at his sister.

"But—"

"Now," he shouted, his face contorted into a furious mask.

Kathy had never seen him so angry. With rough hands, he turned her around and shoved her out the barn door. Outside, she shivered in the cold as smoke billowed out of the livery stable. Voices shouted around her, mingling with the cries of frightened animals and the clang of a distant bell. Several men ran toward the barn carrying buckets.

"The hook and ladder boys are coming," one of them shouted to Kathy as he hurried by.

A block away, a dozen men wearing dark leather fire helmets pulled an iron-framed wagon down the street while townspeople gathered along the boardwalk and urged them on. Long ladders, spike-tipped poles, rubber buckets, and iron axes swung back and forth inside the wagon as it rolled along behind the firemen's running feet.

"Hurry," Kathy cried, waving at the barn where smoke rolled out, blacker and thicker than before. David and Frank were still inside.

The fire wagon rolled to a stop in front of the Stone Barn. Snatching buckets and pike poles, the firemen ran inside. Other townsfolk joined the fray, swinging buckets from both hands, but there seemed to be more buckets than water.

Kathy dodged running men and frantic horses as she

strained to spot David or Frank through the smoke. She didn't notice the arrival of a second group of firemen until she tripped over a long hose leading from a cart that looked like a giant hose wheel. Men in white fire helmets and blue flannel shirts scurried around, unwinding the hose from the cart's axle and hooking it up to a fire hydrant.

Water! At last! But was it in time? Kathy bounced anxiously on her feet as she struggled to see through the black haze shrouding the barn. Where was David? And where was Frank?

Through the haze, David and Frank staggered out of the barn supporting the miner between them. He appeared dazed and weak, as if ready to collapse. Several men hurried to help guide the injured man to the boardwalk across the street, where they sat him down. The boys bent over, hands on their knees, and coughed loud and deep, as if they might heave their lungs out. Kathy ran to their side.

"Are you all right?" she asked.

David looked up and nodded. "The fire's out," he said, squeaking out words between retching coughs. "It burned three stalls. I think it was set. Meant to smoke, not flame. A lot of wet stuff."

Kathy remembered the acrid taste of the ammonia-filled smoke and grimaced.

"We were lucky," David continued. "Found it quick. Barn's made of stone." He shook his head and took a deep breath. "The whole place could have burned."

"What about the animals?" Kathy asked.

"Most of them are out," Frank replied. His coughing had quieted faster than David's, but then he hadn't fought the fire. "The firemen are getting the rest and checking for sparks that may have floated into the loft or another stall. Man, you were good," he said to David. "Where did you learn to fight fires?"

David grinned, then was wracked by another fit of coughing.

"From our uncle," Kathy replied, torn between pride and concern. "Our uncle's a smokejumper—does search and rescue, too."

"Really?" Frank said. "I'm impressed."

Kathy looked over at the cluster of men hovering around the miner, who looked considerably ill. He lay back on the boardwalk, holding his head.

"He doesn't seem like a bad guy, does he?" she said, thinking of how hard he had worked to save the barn and horses.

"He's not," David said, his coughs slowing to a manageable hack. "He's not the one. Neither is Rocky Mountain Joe."

"What?" Kathy said.

"He's not?" Frank exclaimed.

"No," David replied. He walked over to the boardwalk and sat down, shoulders slumped and hands hanging limply in his lap.

"There's another guy," he said. "I think he started

the fire. I saw him in the barn before help arrived. It was odd, because he just stood there, not helping. Then, when I went to get some water, he hit the map man with a board, knocking him down. He reached inside the map man's coat and took a piece of paper. I think it was the map. I yelled, but he ran off. I couldn't follow him. Honest, I couldn't." He looked at Kathy and Frank with pleading eyes. "I had to help the map man. He was hurt, but he insisted on fighting the fire. Too worried about the horses, I guess. I couldn't leave him alone, not with blood dripping from his head." David groaned and shook his head. "I lost the real bad guy. I should have known."

"Why?" Kathy asked, touching her brother's arm in sympathy. "How could you have known?"

"The riddle. I didn't pay attention to the riddle. 'Beware the man with a golden smile, whose heart is black and filled with guile. He'll steal a map from an honest man, through fire and smoke and sleight of hand.' The map man was the honest man. But what the heck is a golden smile?"

Frank sat beside David on the boardwalk, his own shoulders sagging in defeat.

"Did you get a look at the guy?" he asked. "Would you recognize him if you saw him?"

"I got a good look, all right," David replied, rubbing his forehead and pushing back his brown hair, now slightly stiff from smoke and grit. "I just don't know where to find him. We're right back where we started."

Kathy sank to the boardwalk and, elbows on her knees, she cupped her chin in her hands. Glumly, she watched the firemen clean up the smoky mess while other men rounded up loose horses and mules and took them down the street. She was tired and miserable and her muscles were stiff and sore from her hard labor. A day had gone by and they still didn't know where to find the man with the golden smile. Would she have to work at the Brainard again? She dreaded the idea. Surely things couldn't get worse.

Or could they? Kathy sat up as two men approached with determined strides. In the smoldering light, a badge glinted on the shorter man's chest.

"You there," he said, as the pair stopped in front of Frank. "Mr. Simpson here says you were in the barn when the fire started." Frank rubbed his hands on his jeans and swallowed hard.

"Yes, sir," he replied. "I was to watch the barn."

"Well, ya didn't do too good a job, now, did ya?"

Mr. Simpson held up his hand as if to call the other man off. "Frank," he said, "I need to know what happened—so does the constable."

There was a long moment of silence, then David, Frank, and Kathy all began to talk at once. It took Mr. Simpson's firm voice to quiet things down enough so that each person could talk, one at a time. Mr. Simpson listened, impassively, giving no hint of his thoughts, while the constable frowned. Kathy was sure they were all going to be arrested.

"I'll have to check your stories out in the morning," the constable growled. "Meanwhile, I'm tempted to throw you all in jail."

Mr. Simpson cleared his throat. "That won't be necessary. I heard the boys worked hard to save the horses and fight the fire. That counts for something. I'm moving the animals to the livery across from the Brainard for the night and I made arrangements for the children to stay there, too, if they want—as long as they stay away from the lamps."

"But we didn't do it," Kathy blurted out.

The constable raised an eyebrow in a threatening glare. Kathy bit her lip, holding down her indignation.

"No lamps," Frank said quickly, nudging Kathy with his elbow. "Promise."

Mr. Simpson considered them for a long moment, then nodded. "Then off with you," he said. He turned and walked away.

The constable gave the trio one last piercing look, then hurried to join Mr. Simpson. "I tell you, the rascals should be locked up until we know for sure," he said.

Frank grabbed both David's and Kathy's hands. "Let's get out of here before Mr. Simpson changes his mind."

"We need to get our things," David said, looking

down at his feet. "I've got to get my boots." Kathy looked down at her own stockinged toes, just now remembering she didn't have on shoes.

"Clothes, too," she added, "and the food—if it's not ruined."

"Then let's go," Frank said. "And hurry." He led the way, skirting around men loading poles and buckets back onto the fire wagon. The three were halfway across the street when David stopped.

"Wait!" he called to Frank, who was several steps ahead. "Come here." He pointed into the dark. "Over there. See that guy? He's the man who stole the map."

Kathy strained to see through the smoky haze that muffled the moonlight. She saw a barrel-shaped man standing on the boardwalk not far from the Stone Barn. He leaned against an awning post, watching all the commotion. There was something familiar about him. "Let's get closer," she said. "I think I've seen him before."

They worked their way down the street, keeping behind the fire wagon and hose cart as long as possible, then slowly sauntered past the man. He shifted position and moved into the light from a nearby window. Kathy caught her breath. She recognized the man. She remembered the receding hairline, the squinty eyes, and the greasy mustache that curled into his mouth when he smiled. Mostly she remembered the nose hair.

"Gross," she said. "It's that man with the long. . . ."

Her words trailed off as the man turned and looked her way. He curled his upper lip into a snarling smile as if he, too, recognized her and the boys and dared them to come his way. He took a step toward them and raised his lip higher. A spark of lamplight glinted off a large front tooth. Kathy stepped back, her eyes opened wide. She now remembered the dull yellow glimmer, all but hidden behind his greasy mustache.

"The golden smile," she whispered. She turned and tugged David and Frank away from the thief, back toward the other side of the street and the safety of a small group of men. "He's the man with the golden smile," she hissed.

"What do you mean?" David asked, resisting Kathy's pull.

Kathy tugged harder. "I waited on him. He was at the table next to the map man. He must have heard everything. David, I think he has a gold tooth. It's the golden smile."

"The golden smile," David said. He turned and stared at the man, who began to wander down the street. David watched as if entranced, then he set his mouth in the same determined look he had whenever he charged the other soccer team's goalie and kicked a winning score. "This time we won't lose him."

10 Wagons Ho!

"David, Kathy, wake up!" Frank's muffled voice shouted from below. "Hurry! He's gone!"

"What?" Kathy pushed herself up on her elbows. Her mind felt foggy and slow from too little sleep. She blinked in confusion at the dimly lit loft with its piles of hay and the figure of her brother spread out under a horse blanket. Irritably, she pushed at the itchy, yellow bits of chaff that stuck in her hair and clung to her apron, petticoat, and dress. Then she rubbed her nose and sniffed. The smell of horse, ash, and soot on her smoke-smudged clothes jogged her memory and she sat up in alarm.

"David, wake up!"

They couldn't lose the bad guy, the thief in the night. Not again!

They had been so careful, keeping out of sight, as they followed the man back to the Brainard Hotel. David had been obsessed, like a bloodhound on the scent, following the man through the parlor and right up the stairs to Room Five. He would have camped out at the doorstep, too, if Kathy and Frank hadn't pulled him away and dragged him to the nearby livery.

"David, wake up!" Kathy jerked the horse blanket off her brother and roughly shook him. "That Crockett guy is gone!"

Talbot Crockett. Registered in Room Five. Kathy had checked. While Frank had tugged David out the front door of the Brainard, she had flipped open the hotel's registry, a large, gray book with red binding that sat on the parlor desk. It was two inches thick and full of signatures from travelers and dinner guests, but she knew where to look. Talbot Crockett. And now he was gone.

David bolted upright. "What?" he said, shaking his head and sending flecks of hay everywhere. Not bothering to put on his boots, he scrambled over to the edge of the loft. "What do you mean, gone?"

"What I said," Frank replied, peering up from the shadows of the livery barn. "He just got on the stagecoach and left. How long were you guys going to sleep anyway?"

"Long?" Kathy grumbled as she grabbed her black leather shoes and tugged them on. It seemed like she had fallen asleep only moments ago. She ran her fingers through her hair, combing it with one hand while she brushed hay off her dress with the other. She tried to smooth the crinkles and smudges out of her clothes, wishing now she had stripped down to chemise and underdrawers before crawling between the blankets. But she had been too tired and the night had felt cold after the heat of the fire.

"Why didn't you wake us up?" David snapped, slapping chaff off his coat and jeans and tugging on his boots. He slid down the wooden ladder in one smooth glide, with Kathy stepping carefully behind. The livery smelled of sour manure. It wasn't as clean as the Stone Barn and already the air was thick with black flies. Except for the hum of buzzing wings, however, the barn was quiet. The snuffling and *harrumphs* that had lulled Kathy to sleep were gone. Doors hung open to empty stalls.

"Where are all the horses?" she asked.

A smug look crept onto Frank's face. "You guys sleep like logs," he said as he leaned against a rail and stuck his hands in his jeans pockets. "Didn't you hear anything?"

Kathy shook her head, slapping at a fly that seemed attracted to the bits of hay in her hair. David pursed his lips tight in silent anger.

"Logs," Frank muttered and then continued. "The horses and mules are gone. Some were taken back to the Stone Barn and some hitched up to the wagons. Remember all those loaded wagons in the street last night?"

Images of wagons piled high with large pieces of equipment, boxes, and other freight popped into

Kathy's mind. They had been strung along the street like beads on a necklace.

"They're gone now," Frank said. His face flushed with color as his eyes brightened into a smile. "It was great! Did you know the strongest horses are hitched next to the wheels and do most of the work? That's why they're called 'wheels.' And mules are stronger than horses. And freighters can only use four or six horses to haul a wagon up the canyon because of all the sharp curves." Words tumbled out of his mouth as his hands danced in the air.

"Stop," David said, interrupting Frank mid-stroke. "What about the guy, Talbot Crockett?"

"The Nose," Kathy interjected, grimacing at the memory of long black nose hairs.

Frank's chest fell. "Him. Right. Well, I was helping some guys hitch up their teams when the stagecoach arrived." His lips parted into a toothy grin. "Just like in the movies, with the driver up front, foot on the brake, hands holding the reins." He flicked an imaginary whip in the air.

"Frank!" Kathy groaned.

"Oh, all right," he grumbled. "The Nose got on the stagecoach and left."

David slapped the palm of his hand against a wooden support beam. "If you had let me stay by his door, this wouldn't have happened," he snapped

Frank snorted. "You sleep like a rock. He'd have stepped right over you."

David growled and paced up and down the stable floor, his boots swirling up dust from the hard-packed ground.

"Where did the stage go? We have to follow The Nose."

"Up the canyon," Frank answered with a grin. "Just like the riddle says. 'Up Boulder Canyon all choked with dust, he will pursue his own gold lust.' It was the Caribou stage. It goes to Nederland and Caribou."

David sat on a crate with a *thunk*. He crossed his arms and scowled. Kathy could feel a black wall of frustration settle around him. She turned away, too tired to deal with it, and tugged at the stocking that kept slipping down her leg.

Frank didn't seem happy now either. His eyes narrowed as he stuck his hands back in his pockets and hunched his shoulders. "You're not the only one with a riddle, you know," he said.

Kathy looked over at her brother. "He's right, David," she said. "You solved your riddle. We know who the man is. We'll find him again. Won't we, Frank?"

"Right," Frank replied, a little more cheerfully than was needed.

David dug the toe of his boot into the floor. Then, uncrossing his arms, he took a deep breath. "You're right," he finally said. "It's just—I keep hearing the riddle over and over again in my head. It's driving me nuts. It's almost like a headache. I've got to follow him.

I've just got to. Where do you think he went, Nederland or Caribou?"

"I don't know," Frank said with a shrug. "Nederland comes first. It's twenty minutes up the canyon—in a car, that is. Caribou's farther. It's an old ghost town—it will be an old ghost town," he corrected himself. "My family went hiking there once. Not much to see. Just an old cemetery and some stone walls. There's a bunch of mines, too, but there're mines everywhere in these mountains."

Caribou—Kathy rolled the word around on her tongue. Didn't the map man say something about Caribou? She couldn't quite remember. She scratched her ankle under the unfastened shoes and fumbled with their tiny buttons, trying to latch them with her fingers. She tried three buttons, then gave up. "Frank, can I borrow your knife?"

He pulled out his pocketknife and tossed it on the ground by her feet. She opened the screwdriver blade with the hook and latched the first button.

David smacked his leg with his fist. "We've got to follow The Nose," he said. "'To right a wrong and end my shame, follow this man who is to blame.' We've got to move—now!" He jumped up and strode out of the stable.

Kathy and Frank exchanged startled glances. She quickly finished latching her shoes and gave Frank his knife. Together, they hurried after David. They found him standing still and rigid in the middle of the street.

"Okay," he said through clenched teeth. "I don't know what to do next." He turned to Frank. "What does your riddle say? I can only remember mine."

Frank cleared his throat. "'Up to the No Name he will flee to seek and steal the missing key. Up Boulder Canyon all choked with dust, he will pursue his own gold lust. All script in bronze he'll find the key, not meant to satisfy man's greed. It opens more than just a map, the Otherworld lies at its lap.'"

A puzzled frown crossed David's face. "What does it mean, 'up to the No Name'?"

"I don't know," Frank answered. "Maybe it's a place that doesn't have a name. Or a place that you can't say the name, or a place that you shouldn't say the name, like 'the place that can't be named.' It could be anything—a mountain peak, a valley, a stream." He kicked a clod of dirt and scowled. "Why couldn't that old dwarf just tell us?"

Kathy turned and stared down the dusty road that snaked its way up the canyon.

"At least we know he went to Nederland," Kathy offered.

"But how do we get there?" David asked.

No one had an answer.

"Hello!" A familiar voice broke the silence. "Did you find your Uncle Bob?" Rocky Mountain Joe strolled toward them, fringes of leather swishing back and forth along the sleeves of a buckskin jacket and the leggings of buckskin pants. He stopped in front of the trio, his eyes glinting at them from under a wide-brimmed leather hat. Frank's mouth dropped open while David stared owl-eyed.

"Uh, yeah," David said. "We did, but we lost him."

"Lost him?" Joe's lips twitched into a smile. "That should be an interesting story."

"Honest," David said. "We did lose him. He was at the Brainard, but he took the stagecoach this morning before . . . well, before some of us got up."

"But we know his name," Frank blurted, grinning broadly. "Crockett, Talbot Crockett."

Joe tweaked an eyebrow at Frank. "Uncle Bob's name is Talbot Crockett?"

"*Robert* Talbot Crockett," David said, jabbing Frank with an elbow.

"Staff," Frank quickly added.

Joe chuckled. "Robert Talbot Crockett Staff it is. Still. . . ." He hooked a thumb on his belt, next to a leather-fringed pouch with colored beads sewn on its side. "You might have talked to him *yesterday.*"

David floundered for an answer.

"We weren't sure how he'd react," Kathy said, stepping forward. "You see, we don't really know him. We thought we should wait—maybe learn a little bit about him first. After all, what if he's mean?"

"Yeah," Frank said. "What if he's a bad guy or something?"

"I see," Joe said. "And how do you plan to find him now?"

David's face brightened. "You're going up the canyon, aren't you? Couldn't we come with you?"

Joe stroked his goatee as if contemplating the thought. "I reckon so," he finally said. "I'm catching a ride with Gus Farrow. He's hauling hay to Caribou and I imagine he won't mind if you ride in the back. I'm meeting him here in an hour. We can ask him then. You three had breakfast?"

Kathy's stomach growled as she shook her head. She grimaced at the thought of eating the smoky biscuits and potatoes hidden in the hay.

"Best you get down to George's place for a quick bite. Tell him the meal's on me. Now git," Joe said, waving them away.

Nobody argued, least of all Frank, who practically skipped along.

"Did you see that?" he asked, eyes sparkling. "He's just like Buffalo Bill Cody."

"Buffalo who?" Kathy asked, trying to keep up.

"Buffalo Bill Cody."

"Who's that?"

Neither David nor Kathy had ever heard of him.

"Don't you guys know anything?" Frank said with a snort. "Haven't you heard of the Wild West Show? Annie Oakley? Wild Bill Hickok?"

Each time, David and Kathy shook their heads.

"I don't believe it," Frank said, rolling his eyes. "Where did you move from, anyway?" He didn't wait for a response. Instead, he half-skipped faster, leaving Kathy and David to catch up. Ignoring the strange looks of the folks around them, he whistled a Western tune.

George greeted them more warmly this time. He had heard about the fire. "An extra treat," he said as he served them bacon and eggs with their pancakes.

"We should probably buy some food," David said, when they had finished their meal and stepped back into the street. "While we've got the chance. I earned some nickels yesterday sweeping the boardwalk for one of the hotels and washing down a carriage after some boys flicked mud wads at it." He reached into his pocket and pulled out several coins. "What about you guys?"

Kathy jingled the change in her apron pocket, then reached in and handed it to David. Frank added the wages he had earned from Mr. Simpson. Together, they had almost two dollars.

"It's not a lot, but it's a start," David said, eyeing the small pile in his hand.

They agreed that Kathy would go back to the livery stable to collect the bundles of clothes and food they had squirreled away while Frank and David headed for the open shops. Kathy wished she could go, too, but her feet already hurt. The walk to the stable was enough.

She gathered their supplies and sat down next to the building. While she waited, she picked up a stick and sketched in the dirt. She wondered if her parents missed them. Wondered if they'd ever get home. With each thought, she pressed her stick deep into the soil, scratching out the shape of a tree. She had just finished drawing the trunk and long drooping limbs that arched to the ground when Frank and David came jabbering down the street.

"One dollar," Frank crowed. He held up a can of peaches the size of a small football in his right hand while cradling two in his left arm. "Five for one dollar! And look how big they are. We're set for two or three days. Especially with the biscuits, cheese, and potatoes."

"Two or three days," Kathy said. "I hope it doesn't take that long." She desperately wanted to go home.

Frank piled the cans beside her and grinned. "I hope it takes a month. And look," he said, slipping his hand into a pocket. He pulled out the clear glass marble with the silver figure of an eagle inside. "I couldn't help buying it. It's like finding a treasure. Better than that stupid bowl in the incinerator."

David dropped two more cans onto the cache of food, then reached out to examine the marble. "I don't think I've ever seen one like that," he said, rolling the sphere between his fingers and thumb before giving it back.

Kathy smiled at the pleasure on Frank's face, then turned back to scratch at the ground. She had just added a tangled mass of roots to her tree when a sturdy wagon pulled by four mules trundled down the street, loaded high with hay. A large black dog trotted beside the wagon, a slobbery tongue lolling out of its mouth. Rocky Mountain Joe and another man sat on the front seat, chatting over the squeak of the wagon wheels. The wagon pulled to a stop in front of the trio.

"Climb on up," Joe said. "Gus has a light load today. He'll haul you to Nederland if you like. Gus, meet Kathy, David, and Frank."

Gus nodded curtly, bobbing a battered hat that was pocked with bumps and stains from years of wear. "You boys, in the back," he said. "The little lady sits up front with us."

"That's not fair," Frank complained. One sharp look from Gus and he quickly closed his mouth and headed for the back of the wagon.

Kathy reached for the wagon seat, then stopped as her tight sleeves threatened to tear and the bodice of her

dress inched up her chest. "Oh, bother," she mumbled as she tugged the dress back down. "Who designed these things anyway?"

Gus slid off the wagon and lifted her up. He grabbed the food and the bundles of clothes, tossed them to Joe, then climbed aboard the wagon and sat on Kathy's right.

Rocky Mountain Joe reached behind the seat and pulled out three hats—two battered felt hats and a slightly ratty straw one with a red ribbon tied around it. He tossed the felt hats back to the boys and handed the straw one to Kathy.

"Best put these on," he said. "Compliments of the church. You'll burn without them."

Kathy adjusted the hat on her head, letting the ribbon hang down her back. Gus nodded and smiled. He picked up the harness lines and gave them a snap.

"Get up," he said.

11 Up Boulder Canyon

With a lurch, the wagon rolled toward the rugged peaks that rose abruptly out of the plains. The wheels squeaked and groaned in rhythm to the jangle of the harness bell that hung between the two lead mules, while the hay loaded in back swayed with each dip in the rutted ground. Kathy clung to her seat, wondering if the road would get better.

"How far to Nederland?" she asked.

"Good part of a day," Joe replied. "Faster if you're on a stagecoach."

Kathy wiggled in her seat and tried to get more comfortable.

They had gone only a short way when Gus slowed the wagon to a stop. At the mouth of Boulder Canyon, a weathered, peak-roofed tollhouse stood guard, exacting tribute for use of the road. Gus dug into his pocket and pulled out some change: $1.00 for the wagon and two mules, $.25 each for the two extra animals.

"That's highway robbery," David complained as he

watched the wagoner pay the toll. "This is a public road and it's not even very good." Gus tilted his head and squinted back at David.

"This here's a mountain road, boy, built by private interests. We're lucky to have a road at all. Besides," he said, snapping the lines to start the mules, "I've seen worse."

Almost as soon as they entered the canyon, Kathy understood why the trip would take so long. The mules tugged and strained up sharp inclines while steep granite walls stretched high into the sky on both sides. Slapping along the edge of the narrow road and splattering against large boulders squatting in its path, a turbulent creek twisted and turned its way down the mountain.

Every now and then, a granite slab of rock would jut into the water, blocking passage and forcing the road to cross the creek on a low wooden bridge. Joe said there were thirty-three bridges between Boulder and Nederland. David and Frank began to keep count.

Sometimes a bridge wouldn't work. Sometimes the canyon walls hugged the creek too closely on both sides to allow for a road. Then the wagon would trundle across a man-made ledge of stone, logs, and earth straddling the line between rock and water. Each time, Kathy would grip the wooden seat beneath her, fearful the cribwork ledge would give way and tumble them into the frothing stream. Once, when a ledge was particularly scary, she glanced back and saw Frank grinning with joy, while David looked only slightly nervous.

When they weren't crossing bridges or cribwork ledges, however, the journey up the canyon was pleasant enough. They frequently greeted other wagons hauling ore and freight down the mountain to Boulder. Once a stagecoach dashed by. At these encounters, the down-hill wagon would usually pull over into a small turnout to allow Gus to pass. The road was too narrow for two vehicles at once. Even with the turnouts, passing was tight. Gus often had to inch the wagon close to the rocky edge that dropped into the stream. Kathy tried not to watch, tried not to hold her breath.

Most of the time, however, she gazed about and marveled at the canyon. It rose like a cathedral of green, rust, brown, and gray domed by a sky of vivid blue. Douglas fir and ponderosa pine clung to the rocky walls while thick patches of chokecherry, gooseberry, and river birch crowded the edge of the stream. Splashes of yellow, blue, and white speckled the road's border where delicate flowers bobbed their heads. They reminded Kathy of Mrs. Acheson's backyard.

"Beautiful, isn't it?" Joe said. He inhaled deeply, then let out a long slow breath. "Smell those pines and the mountain air. I like to come here often to clear out the noise of the city. And there's so much beauty to draw."

"You sketch?" Kathy asked, thrilled that she and Joe had something in common.

"Yep," he replied. "I sure do. And sometimes I write a poem or two." He opened a medium-sized journal and flipped through the pages. Inside, delicate pictures crafted in black ink adorned the paper, with neat descriptions written underneath. Occasionally the evenly spaced lines of a poem would flash by. Rocky Mountain Joe stopped on a page where fine, crisscrossed lines etched out a thundering waterfall shadowed by towering rock. He tapped the picture with his finger. "Boulder Falls! It's the most romantic place I've ever seen." He smiled at Kathy. "Just like a lovely young lady."

128

Kathy felt herself turn red. Out of the corner of her eye, she saw Frank roll over and clutch his throat, mouth wide open and tongue hanging out, while David shook with quiet laughter. In disgust, she turned her back so she couldn't see the boys.

"I draw sometimes, too," she said. She stared down at her hands, rubbing the fingers together. Would she ever see her drawings again or feel the smooth edge of her colored pencils? What would Joe think of her special white eraser or her spiral bound sketchpad with the perforated edges? Would he have liked her drawing of a chestnut tree with a knobby-nosed face half-hidden in the bark? She took a deep breath, looked up, and smiled.

"How will you get back to Boulder?"

"I'll pitch camp somewhere," he replied, patting a bedroll tucked behind the wooden seat. "I'll walk down in the morning. I like the peace of the mountains, the stillness of the night, and the twinkle of the stars."

Kathy groaned. "Not me," she said in a low tone so the boys wouldn't hear. "The dark scares me."

Rocky Mountain Joe tilted his head and gave a quizzical look from under his leather hat. "I reckon that's because you imagine bad things in the dark. Think of its beauty and wonders, instead: the call of the nighthawk in the fading sky; the roar of its wings as it dives for an evening meal; crickets calling back and forth; laughing coyotes as they sing their melodies; the hooting of the owl; or the brilliance of the stars and moon. Without the night and its cloak of darkness, we would miss these wonderful things."

"What about ghosts and goblins and—well, other things?"

Joe laughed. "Can't say I've run into any of them. Leastwise, none that I can't handle," he added with a wink.

"I have," Kathy mumbled to herself.

With each curve of the canyon, the sun grew hotter and the wooden seat felt more like stone. They crossed bridge after bridge, as the road wound its way up the mountain. Occasionally, they passed a mining shack clinging to the canyon walls, and at one branch in the canyon they passed a small town with mills, shops, mines, and houses squeezed along a stream that rushed to join Boulder Creek. Farther up, where a gulch joined the canyon, the road split as a track meandered south toward the mining town of Magnolia. The mules plodded on, following the main canyon road.

By mid-afternoon, when they had almost reached Boulder Falls, Kathy felt a shiver run up her spine. She hugged her arms tight to her chest and glanced around the canyon walls. Without saying a word, she scooted closer to Rocky Mountain Joe.

At the turn by Boulder Falls, Gus pulled the wagon to a stop. "May as well rest the animals here and enjoy the scenery."

Joe hopped off the wagon. "Come on," he said,

beckoning to Kathy, David, and Frank. "You can barely see the falls from here."

Scrambling over rocks, he led them into a side canyon carved by another stream. With each step, the roar of the water grew louder until at last they reached the falls: seventy feet of thundering fury that boiled to a froth on the rocks below. Green mosses cushioned the water's edge while delicate ferns dipped their heads under overhanging banks.

Joe nodded toward the ferns. "Someday I'll write a poem about them. And look at that," he said, pointing out the silhouette of a large horned owl tucked in the branches of a tree. "Quiet, now. Let's not disturb him."

He flipped out his sketchbook and leaned against a boulder. With pencil in hand, he scratched quick, sharp lines on the paper, bringing the sleeping owl to life on the page. Kathy watched in fascination, marveling at the speed and grace of each stroke. With a final dab, Joe finished the owl, its body half-hidden behind the branches of a pine tree. Beneath the picture, he signed his initials, then wrote 'Remember the wonders of the night.' Carefully he tore the page out of the sketchbook and handed it to Kathy along with two blank pages.

"Don't forget," he said, tapping her nose lightly with a finger. He closed his sketchbook and tucked it under his arm. "Best we be heading back." He stood and called to the boys who had climbed closer to the falls and were tossing stones into the foaming water. Then, with a wink, he turned away, and headed toward the wagon.

Kathy traced the delicate outline of the owl with her finger, then gently covered the drawing with the two extra pages. Careful not to crumple the papers, she slipped them into her apron pocket.

"What's that?" David asked as he scrambled down the rocks to join Kathy.

"Nothing," she answered.

With the rattle of scattering pebbles, Frank slid down the rocky slope and landed with a *thud* beside her. "I've been here before," he said. "Only the falls are smaller and there's a walking trail now, with steps and everything. I like it better this way." He glanced over at the receding back of Rocky Mountain Joe. "He didn't write a poem, did he?" he asked, a troubled look on his face. "Indian scouts are supposed to be tough."

"He is tough," Kathy said, with a huff. "Tough guys can write poetry, too." Flipping her hair behind her shoulders, she turned her back on the boys and scrambled back toward the wagon.

They didn't leave right away. Gus said it was as good a spot as any to eat.

"Finally," Frank said, jumping into the wagon and snatching the box of food. The biscuits were stale, the potatoes cold, and the cheese just a little bit runny. Everything smelled of smoke. But Kathy still thought the food looked better than whatever it was Joe and Gus had.

After inhaling several biscuits, Frank grabbed a can of peaches to open with his knife. Before he cut the lid, he changed his mind. "We better save it for later," he said, putting it back in the hay.

When the meal was finished, Joe grabbed his bedroll from the wagon. "Here's where I get off," he said. "I just might draw those ferns. Good luck with your journey. I hope you find whoever it is you're looking for. And remember, you owe me a story or two—someday."

Kathy's chest tightened. She had trouble catching her breath. She had felt safe with Joe. With him around, things didn't seem so strange or frightening. But now they would be on their own again. Forcing a weak smile, she said goodbye. Joe smiled back, then shook hands with David and Frank. Nodding a final farewell, he swung his bedroll over his back, then strolled down the road. Frank stared after him, a mixture of emotions mirrored on his face. Kathy didn't want to watch. She turned away and pulled herself up onto the wagon seat, then climbed into the hay behind it. She had had enough of the hard wooden seat. The boys could sit with Gus. Besides, Frank seemed to need a treat.

At first, they rode along in awkward silence. Gus wasn't the talkative sort, and Frank was unusually quiet. Soon, however, Frank asked a question, and before long he and Gus were busy discussing mules and freighting. Gus showed Frank how to drive the mules, explaining which ones were the leaders and which were the haulers.

133

"See that there lead mule, Betty?" Gus pointed to the front mule on the left. "See how she perks her ears? She's listening real close, paying attention. She can hear another wagon's bell a mile away and if she don't hear it, Dog does. I know when a wagon's coming by how she cocks her ears. She's a smart ol' gal. That's why she's in front. She shows the other mules what to do and where to go. Now Bessie, there, next to her, is just about as smart. I reckon they're the finest pair of mules this side of the Divide."

The conversation rattled on until Kathy lost interest and lay back in the hay, shading her face with the straw hat. She was just dozing off when excited barking stirred her awake. She peeked out from under the hat and saw Gus sit up straighter, if that was possible, and pull the wagon to a stop. Up the canyon, the low rumble of wheels and the frantic jangle of bells announced the rapid approach of another wagon. Kathy sat up and strained to see through the trees that blocked her view of the turn up ahead.

"What's happening?" she asked.

"Some dang fool's lost his brakes," Gus hissed through gritted teeth. "Or else he's driving too fast."

He glanced around for a way to get off the road, then urged the mules to back up. They seemed to sense the danger and moved at the slightest tug of the lines. Sweat beaded on Gus's face.

"If I tell you kids to jump, you jump off mountain

side and hightail it up the slope, you hear?"

Kathy scrambled over to the back of the seat and huddled behind Frank and David. Frank paled beneath his freckles as he stared up the canyon, while David frantically scanned the steep slope beside them.

The barking grew louder. Soon a wagon loaded high with boxes and heavy equipment skidded around the bend up ahead. The driver, a boy not much older than David, struggled to pull his team of horses back while straining against the brake. Gus cussed loudly, urging his mules to move faster. Closer and closer the wagon thundered. David grabbed Kathy's hand and they were about to jump when the wagon came to a halt. Gus's face blazed red with fury.

"Boy, don't you know to take these roads slow when loaded up like that?" He nodded toward the boxes that looked as if they were about to topple out of the wagon.

The driver's face was a sickly white. "I couldn't hold them down that last pitch. It—it was slippery," he stammered.

"Ain't you got no rough-lock or road shoe, boy?" Gus glanced at the back wheels of the wagon. "I don't see no extra brakes there."

The boy swallowed hard. "I didn't think I'd need them."

"Don't need 'em?" Gus's eyes blazed with fire. "You trying to get yourself killed? You dang near ran over my mules." The boy said nothing as he sat rigid, harness lines quivering in his hands.

Gus grumbled under his breath as he backed his wagon farther down the road to a nearby turnout. When his team was safely at the side of the road, the boy clucked to his horses and drove his wagon forward. He stared straight ahead as he passed.

"Fool," Gus mumbled. "We'll be picking him out of the water some day."

"What do you mean?" Frank asked, his freckles bright spots on his pale cheeks.

Gus hesitated, then answered. "Accidents in these mountains can be real bad," he said, snapping the lines to move the mules back up the road. "Won't ever forget the one last year." He shook his head in memory. "Freighter by the name of Stevens was coming down the canyon about a mile behind me. Good man, Stevens. He was loaded up with ore when his rough-lock broke. Sent that wagon crashing up behind the horses and pushed them right into the creek. You could hear their screams bouncing off the canyon walls miles away." Gus paused a moment. "Then, there was a silence so still it darn near stopped your heart. By the time we got to them, two of the horses were dead. We had to shoot the others."

"What about the driver?" Frank asked, swallowing hard.

"He lived another week," Gus replied. "Some say they've seen his ghost where the accident took place."

Kathy hugged her arms to her chest and shivered. "Was that just below Boulder Falls?" she asked in a tiny voice.

"Yep, sure was," Gus answered. "Guess you already heard about it."

David gave Kathy a funny look, then leaned over toward Frank and poked him in the side. "Still want to drive a mule team?" he asked, a wicked grin on his face. Frank elbowed him back.

Ignoring the boys, Kathy nestled back in the hay. She wished the ride were over. She was glad when David and Frank joined her, lying shoulder to shoulder. Together, they gazed up at the sky as day shaded into dusk and then the pitch black of night.

"Not far now," Gus called over his shoulder.

Kathy stared into the darkness. She had never seen a sky so crisp, the stars like bright diamonds set against the cool black of nothingness. She could almost reach up and touch them. She snuggled deeper into the hay, warm and content. With Gus driving the wagon and Frank and David nearby, the dark didn't seem scary. She thought about Rocky Mountain Joe, and listened closely to hear the call of a coyote or the hoot of an owl. The nighthawks that flitted around the canyon at dusk had already gone to bed. Her eyes drooped lower and lower with the rocking of the wagon. When Gus pulled into Nederland, she was sound asleep.

12 Fool's Gold

A map faded in and out, just beyond Kathy's reach, while two men argued under the sketched branches of an old oak tree. Entangled in the limbs, an eagle screeched at a flapping owl. Kathy woke with a start. Her heart thumped loudly. She needed to grasp something important—but she couldn't remember what.

She rolled over, knocking hay onto her face and into her mouth. With a sputter, she spat the grass out, sat up, and looked around. A pink crack of light etched across the sky behind the rough silhouette of mountains to the east, while the jangle of harnesses and the scuffle of hooves on packed dirt broke the stillness of the brisk, cold air. It was morning and she was still in the wagon.

Pushing aside the coarse blanket that someone had thrown over her, she looked around for the boys. David's head and one arm poked out of the hay as strands around his face fluttered back and forth in rhythm to his snores. Kathy grabbed the exposed arm and shook her brother awake.

"What?" he grumbled, as he sat up and stretched. "Where are we?"

"Nederland," Gus's voice boomed from behind them, making them jump. "Time you three got up. This load's due in Caribou, first thing, and ore is waiting to be hauled back down." He tugged at the brim of his hat, then adjusted the breeching on the mules.

David yawned, then glanced around. "Frank!" he hollered.

"What?" a muffled voice replied, followed by Frank's head popping up out of the hay like a jack-in-the-box. Spikes of sandy hair stuck out in every direction, speckled with bits of greenish-gray. Kathy sniggered, only partially hiding her smile behind her hand.

"What are you laughing at?" Frank said crossly,

140

shaking hay out of his hair. "It's barely light," he said. "What's the deal?"

"It's time to get up," David replied, scrounging around for the cans of peaches and the nearly empty box of biscuits and cheese. "We're in Nederland." He stopped and looked at Frank. "Do we get off?"

Frank blinked at the question and frowned. "I don't know. The Nose . . . uh, Uncle Bob took the Caribou stage, but I didn't hear him say where he was going."

"Is that all you know?" Gus asked, as he finished checking the lines. "Stagecoaches run all over these parts, each connecting with the other. The Caribou stage stops here and at Caribou, but from Nederland other coaches go to Black Hawk, Central City, and Ward. And sometimes the Caribou stage lets folks off down the canyon to catch a ride to Magnolia."

"Magnolia?" Kathy asked. "You mean that turnoff in the canyon?"

"Yep," Gus replied. "That'd be the one."

Kathy felt her heart sink. There were too many possibilities. She rubbed at a dull ache just above her eyes. What was she not remembering? 'So find the man who—'

"He took the Caribou stage," Frank said firmly, interrupting her thought. "I checked twice. He came up Boulder Canyon. That's what the riddle says." He stuck his hands in his pockets and glowered. "He was looking for gold."

Gus shook his head and chuckled. "Ain't they all? Me, freighting suits me just fine."

"Seriously," Frank said. "He was looking for gold—'he will pursue his own gold lust' and something about a place without a name. Are there any gold mines without a name, or maybe with a really weird name? Or maybe a mountain or. . . ." His voice trailed off at the look on Gus's face.

"Boy, there're mines all over these here hills. Gold, silver, telluride—telluride ore's got both gold and silver. Caribou's mainly a silver town, but it's got gold, too. Darn near every mine does and each one's got a name. Ain't you got more to go on than that?"

Glumly, Frank shook his head.

"You're in a bind, then, ain't you," Gus said. "Tell you what, the stagecoach is running from Caribou this morning. Why don't you wait here and ask the driver if he's seen your uncle? Might be able to tell you where he got off."

Unable to come up with another suggestion, the boys gathered the food and their bundles of clothing and jumped off the wagon. Slowly, Kathy climbed down, still rubbing her head. She couldn't help but feel they were missing something important.

Gus hauled himself up onto the wagon seat. "I got to git, now," he said. "Good luck to you." He nodded goodbye and snapped the lines.

Kathy watched as the wagon disappeared up the

road, then leaned against the wall of the livery stable and slid to the ground. She wished her headache would go away.

"Here," Frank said, passing her a biscuit. He pulled out his knife and cut a jagged edge along the top of a can of peaches and pried the lid up. Together, the trio munched on biscuits, cheese, and peaches, taking turns dunking the rock-hard bread into the peach juice. Kathy began to feel a little better.

"Let's check out the hotels," David said, after rinsing his hands in the nearby stream. "Maybe someone saw The Nose."

Kathy shook her head. "You go," she said. "I'll watch for the stage." There wasn't much to Nederland anyway: a handful of stores lining one block of the main street; a scattering of weathered, wooden houses that littered the mountain valley; and a large, square building that squatted on the banks of Boulder Creek, spewing yellow tailings into the once-clear waters and swirling black smoke into the crisp mountain air. Kathy didn't think the answer to the riddle was here.

"Watch our stuff, then," David said, as he and Frank wandered off.

She picked up a stick and again traced the outline of a tree in the dirt. Long, scraggly limbs arched down toward the tree's trunk while roots stretched up toward the sky. She frowned at the image. It made no sense. With a brush of the stick, she scribbled it away, then poked at a big, black bug crawling in a nearby tuft of grass. She tried to remember everything she had heard at the Brainard Hotel. She recited her riddle in her head, over and over again. 'To save this man you may be late' spun through her brain. They were running out of time. She was sure of it.

She was still poking at the black bug, when David and Frank skidded to a halt beside her. "We didn't find a thing," David said, tapping her to get up. "Stage is coming, though. Come on, we need to get to the Nederland House."

All three grabbed the food and bundles of clothes and ran to the nearby hotel as the stagecoach thundered into town, its crowded carriage bouncing behind four black horses. Bearded faces stared out of its windows. Five passengers clung on top, each holding onto his hat with one hand and to the piled luggage with the other. The driver, a yellow-haired man with a bushy mustache, pulled the harness lines with a "Whoa" and pressed the brake on the right side of the coach with his polished boot. Dust billowed up and engulfed Kathy as the stage rolled to a stop in front of the Nederland House.

The horses puffed and foamed from their race down the mountain. The driver hopped from his perch and strode into the hotel, his black coat flapping behind him. He returned shortly, holding a stack of letters and a small box. "Loading up," he hollered, as he handed the letters and the box to a man sitting on the front seat.

"Sir," David said, stopping the driver before he climbed aboard. "We're looking for someone who took the stage from Boulder yesterday. We thought you might remember where he got off."

"Maybe," the driver said. "What did he look like? I don't pay much attention to names."

"He has a mustache and is losing his hair," David said, pointing to his forehead.

"And a gold tooth," Frank added, tapping his right front tooth.

"And big nose hairs," Kathy blurted before clapping her hand over her mouth.

The driver burst out laughing. "That's a description worth watching for, but I'm afraid I can't help. I don't look *that* closely at my customers and most folks wear a hat." He pulled himself up onto the front seat. He gathered his lines and cracked a long whip in the air. The horses lurched to a trot and soon the stagecoach disappeared behind a trail of dust.

"What do we do now?" David moaned.

Frank cleared his throat. "I've been thinking," he said. "Instead of searching for The Nose, we should figure out where he's going. That's my riddle," he added with a grin. "It says 'he will pursue his own gold lust.' He's got to be going to a gold mine—after all, he stole the map."

"But the map is for gold in Wyoming," David objected.

For a moment, Frank seemed stumped.

"It doesn't matter," Kathy said. "He stole the map, didn't he? Just like the riddle said. Something about the map is important. Maybe it's—"

"Gold lust, that's what it is," Frank interrupted. "He's looking for a gold mine—only one that's closer, one without a name, or a name you can't pronounce, or—well, something. 'Up to the No Name he will flee, to seek and steal the missing key.'" He turned to David. "I say we look for the mine. We've lost The Nose."

"Key?" Kathy said. "Did you say 'missing key'? You didn't mention that before."

Frank shrugged. "I did up on the bluff."

Kathy groaned in exasperation. "You know we can't remember each other's parts. My riddle mentions a key, too. 'So find the man who owns the key, a gifted one who hears and sees.' I think we need to find *him*. Maybe he's in Caribou. The map man's got a friend in Caribou."

Frank shook his head. "No, we've got to find the mine. We've got to solve my riddle next. Besides, Gus said Caribou's a silver town. We're looking for gold. The riddle said gold."

Kathy turned to David for support but found none. He stood, arms crossed tight against his chest. He didn't agree with anybody.

"So what now?" she asked in defeat.

"The mill," Frank replied. "Let's go to the mill, that

146

big old building by the creek. Mills process ore. I bet they'll know all the mines around here."

Not really liking the idea, Kathy and David agreed to follow Frank. Kathy took her time, straggling behind the boys. She recited her riddle to herself and struggled to remember the conversation she had overheard at the Brainard Hotel. What was it the map man had said? Did he mention a key? She didn't think so, but with each step it became harder to think. The ground beneath her feet shook in rhythm to a rapid *thud-crunch* that pounded louder and louder against her eardrums, nearly drowning out a low, muffled roar.

Annoyed at the distraction, Kathy looked up. Before her towered a monstrous wooden building that sprawled down the slope to the creek. Smoke and steam spewed from tall iron chimneys that sprouted out of the roof like horns on a dragon's head. Kathy sucked in her breath. They were walking into the mouth of a roaring beast.

Frank studied the mill, with its five floors terraced up the slope. Turning, he headed for the top floor, following a wiry man who pushed an iron cart full of rock into the dark interior.

Inside, the man tipped the cart, toppling its load onto a metal scale. Nearby, a large, husky man shoveled stone from sorting bins onto a slanted platform that looked like a giant sieve. Smaller rocks fell through the perforated platform and dropped with a crash onto a steep chute below, while the larger stones rolled down into the gaping maw of a large machine that crunched and chewed them into smaller pieces. Behind the crusher, Kathy could see the tips of large rods rising and falling rapidly, stamping in rhythm to the *thud-crunch* that deafened her ears. The heat and noise were overwhelming.

The husky man stopped shoveling when he spied the trio inside the doorway.

"What are you doing in here?" he shouted over the thundering stamps. "It's dangerous. You want to fall down the grizzly?" He waved his arm toward the rocks cascading down the chute. "Out!" he hollered.

Kathy didn't need more encouragement. She bee-lined out the door, glad to go. The pounding and shaking jarred her nerves and added to the pain in her head. David followed, but Frank stood his ground.

"We just want to ask a question," he shouted.

The man laid down his shovel and walked over. Kathy couldn't hear the conversation but could tell by Frank's gestures that it wasn't going well. The man kept shaking his head until at last Frank's shoulders slumped and he turned away.

"'Mines always got a name,'" he mimicked as he reached the door.

"Well, that was a bust," David snorted as they walked back toward the main road. "Great idea."

"You got a better one?" Frank snapped.

"Yeah," David said. "We've got to find The Nose. He

148

could have taken another stage—that's what we ought
to check. What did Gus say? Central City? Black Hawk?
Maybe The Nose went to Magnolia."

Frank rolled his eyes. "Right."

"Hey, it's better than chasing down some mine without a name," David retorted, slapping at a willow branch
that struggled to grow in the scarred land surrounding
the mill. "Of which, by the way, there doesn't appear
to be one."

Kathy gritted her teeth against the throb in her head.
They had wasted half a day. The Nose was a whole day
ahead of them. Time was running out. 'To save this man
you may be late.' 'A gifted man who hears and sees.'
'So find the man who owns the key.' A missing key—a
missing piece of the map! Kathy remembered the hotel
conversation! The pain in her head subsided. The map
man's friend had a missing piece of the map.

"We've got to go to Caribou," she said.

"Caribou? No way," David said. "We already
checked—"

"Stop!" Kathy cried in exasperation. "We lost The
Nose. We can't find the mine. We don't even know if it
is a mine. We have to find the gifted one. We have got
to find him *now*."

"Kathy," David began, in a condescending tone.

"No, David!" she shouted. "You never listen to me.
This time you listen. We have got to find the gifted one.
He's not here. He's not in Central City. He's in Caribou.

I'm going to Caribou and I don't care who goes with me."
Kathy turned her back on her brother and stomped back
toward the Nederland House and the road to Caribou.
With grim satisfaction, she heard the scramble of feet
behind her, hurrying to catch up.

13 Caribou

Where are they?"

Kathy rubbed her arms and paced back and forth as the setting sun shot orange and red streaks across the sky. It had taken all afternoon to walk the five miles from Nederland to Caribou up a steep, rocky road. With thighs burning from the hike and lungs gasping for breath, the trio had stopped to rest at the outskirts of the small mining town. Then they had split up.

David had wanted to find The Nose. Frank insisted on searching for the unnamed gold mine. Kathy knew she had to find the gifted one—before it was too late.

She stuck her head around the corner of the gray, weathered barn where they had agreed to meet at the end of the day. With eyes leaking tears from the cold, she squinted into the wind that bit her cheeks and whipped red strands of hair out behind her. The boys should have been here by now. In frustration, she turned and kicked at a wooden pole that braced the barn against the western wind. All that did was hurt her toe.

"Watch out!" Frank yelled as he careened around the corner and nearly tumbled into her. Behind him, a short, skinny boy skidded to a halt, dancing lightly to the side to avoid a collision.

"*You* watch out," Kathy said, massaging her toe. She nodded toward the skinny companion. "Who's he?"

Frank draped his arm around the stranger. "This is James Reskelly. He's from Cornwall."

James took off his oversized cap, waved it in the air with a flourish, and bowed. He straightened up and grinned. Mischief twinkled in dark eyes shaded by thick black bangs. "I be helping 'ee find The Nose."

"You're doing what?" Kathy asked. She wasn't sure she had heard James right, not with his strange accent.

"I told him our secret," Frank said with a wink. "I told him The Nose stole some papers from us and we're trying to get them back."

Kathy blinked, surprised, but chose not to say a word—not yet.

Frank leaned against the barn and crossed his arms, a smug look on his face. "So, James is going to help us find him. It's a secret, though," he added in a low, conspiratorial voice. He leaned down, waving Kathy and James closer so they could hear his half-whisper. "After all, if folks found out we were on our own, why, they'd take you away and put you in an orphanage," he said poking Kathy. He straightened up and grinned.

"You jerk," Kathy sputtered, hitting him on his arm. "What about you and David?"

"Too old," he said. He glanced around. "Where is David, anyway?"

"He's not back yet," Kathy replied, "and you're not any older than me."

She glared at Frank as she huddled against the barn, rubbing her arms. She was hungry, she was cold, and, despite the wind, the air stank.

Caribou was a ramshackle collection of unpainted houses, shacks, and shops with a single white, three-story hotel sticking up like a mushroom popping out of the ground. Garbage, manure, and other trash littered the streets, alleys, and yards, their odors mingling with the smell of burning wood that poured from chimneys and from the metal smokestacks of the mines. To add to the noisome mix, rank-smelling outhouses sat haphazardly by almost every building. In a moment of desperation, Kathy had checked one out. The "hole" had been shallow and putrid. She had nearly gagged despite holding her breath and had decided next time she would find a spot in the great outdoors.

She tucked her cold hands under her arms. "Did you find anything?" she asked.

"Naw," Frank replied. "There aren't any gold mines here. Just silver."

"There be gold enough 'ere," James interrupted, sidling up next to Kathy. He grinned at her and winked.

"But silver, now, her be queen."

Kathy looked askance at the skinny boy and edged away. "I didn't have any luck, either. I tried to find 'the gifted one' but every time I went near a mine to ask questions, I got shooed away." She fingered the strands of hair that fluttered in the air. "Something about my hair."

James giggled, and then coughed. "They thought 'ee wanted to go into the bal."

"The what?" Kathy asked, turning her head to hear over the wind.

"The bal," James replied. "The mine. It ain't fitty for a woman to be in the bal. 'Tis bad luck, and 'ee with some fine red 'air. A red-'aired maid be some bad omen."

Kathy glared at James while Frank slapped his leg and hooted into the wind.

"But I ain't moved by such tomfoolery," James said quickly. "'Tis sorry I am if I upset 'ee." He grinned sheepishly. "Frank 'ere said you'm as purty as my sister. He be right."

Kathy's eyes flew open in shocked surprise. Despite the cold, her face grew hot. Frank's laughter suddenly died. It was hard to see in the dusk, but Kathy could swear his face blushed red.

James moved closer and squinted. "What 'ee be speaking of, a gifted one?"

Kathy fidgeted with her apron, brushing unseen lint away to buy time. She didn't want to share everything with James. "Well," she said, dropping bits of invisible fiber to the ground, "I've heard some people can hear things, like in the mines. I was kind of curious."

"Aas," James said, leaning back against the barn and coughing again. "You'm talking about the tommy-knockers. They 'ammer away in the mines. They'll have their fun with 'ee, if 'ee don't treat they right. Me da' swears 'e saw one once. Just like a little old miner he be, with a long salty beard. Didn't say naught, though."

"A little miner?" Frank asked. "Like maybe a short old man with a long gray beard? Maybe dressed in dirty pants and a shirt with rolled-up sleeves?"

"Aas," James replied, "but some be all gold and shimmery like. 'Ee ever see one?"

Avoiding James's inquiring look, Frank stuffed his hands into his pockets. "I've never been in a mine," he said. He glanced oddly at Kathy, before turning to stare out at the mountains. After a moment he cleared his throat. "James knows where we can sleep tonight. There's an empty shack outside of town."

James nodded. "It be empty for years. Not enough work for all the miners who came 'ere a few years back. Caribou ain't big like it be once."

"Big?" Kathy said in surprise. Caribou wasn't more than four or five streets in one direction and two or three in the other, if you ignored the shacks and small, shabby houses scattered along the slopes. It looked to her like Caribou had always been small.

"It's a tiny shack," Frank added, "and we're going to need blankets. It gets cold in the mountains at night, especially this high up, but James says he knows where to get some."

James grinned. "Night shift. A few of the mines be working nights these last weeks. 'Ee can borrow blankets from they who be working."

"How?" Kathy asked.

"Us'll walk in the house and take the blankets. That be all. The men wouldn't mind if 'ee asked, but Frank 'ere said it be a secret. 'Ee just have to get the blankets back by morn."

"Why don't we just stay in the house?" Kathy asked. "Wouldn't that be simpler?"

"If the miners come 'ome early, they'll be finding you," James replied. "It be safer at the empty shack."

Kathy wasn't so sure of that, but she didn't know what else to say. Discouraged, she slid down the barn wall and sat. She tugged her wool stockings up and pulled the lace cuffs of her drawers down in an effort to cover her legs. It was getting colder as night settled down around them and swallowed the mountains up.

"Where's David?" she asked.

As if in answer, her brother turned the corner, hands stuck deep in his coat pockets. "Jeez, it's getting cold," he said, giving his shoulders a shake.

"Any luck?" Frank asked.

156

"No," he replied. "Too many men with receding hair-lines and mustaches. Nobody remembers a gold tooth. We're just going to have to spot him ourselves—if he's here." David looked over at James. "Who's he?"

Frank filled David in. The night shift didn't start for a couple of hours, and James said he had to go home for supper. Promising to return when the mine whistle blew, he hurried up the hill into the darkness.

"We may as well eat," Frank said as James disap-peared. He pulled out his knife and opened a can of peaches—for the third time that day. Wrinkling his nose, he scooped up the slippery mass. "When we get home, I'm never going to eat peaches again."

David snorted in agreement, then stuffed his mouth with a handful. "We've still got a couple of hours," he said. "Let's keep looking when we're done."

They finished the peaches and the few crumbs of bis-cuit and cheese that remained. While the boys waited, Kathy unrolled her bundle of clothes and took out her

157

denim jacket. In the darkness, it didn't matter if she looked strange, and she'd rather be warm. She rolled up her jeans, T-shirt, and button-up shoes and hid them, along with her straw hat, behind the barn. She had already changed to her tennis shoes for the hike up the mountain road. She had had enough of blisters.

"Let's check out the saloons," David suggested when she was ready. "Maybe we'll find The Nose."

They headed up the main street as it climbed toward a large hill pocked with mines. When Kathy had first seen the mines that scarred the mountainside around Caribou, she was aghast at how many there were. Each had a massive mound of broken rock oozing from the mouth of its shaft-house like an open sore in the earth. Around the mines, dead tree stumps littered the hillsides, remnants of the forest that once grew there. But now, all were cloaked in darkness.

Kathy squinted at the buildings along the street, their false fronts creaking in the harsh wind. Several saloons and billiard halls crowded along the block that was "downtown," laughter rolling out of their opened doors while kerosene lights flickered within.

David stopped outside the saloon at the top of the sloping street and turned his back into the wind. "Let's split up," he hollered, trying to be heard over the rushing air. "Frank, you check out that saloon down there, and I'll check out this one."

Frank nodded and faded into the darkness,

holding onto his hat as the wind shoved him down the hill. Kathy drew her jacket closer with fingers stiff from the cold and moved toward the light and noise that leaked through the saloon door. "I'm going inside, too."

Her brother grabbed her arm to hold her back. "You can't. You're a girl."

"So what? I'm cold. I'll freeze out here. I'll just tell them I'm waiting for my uncle." She pulled away and pushed open the door. Warmth washed over her as the smell of cigar smoke, stale beer, and unwashed bodies bombarded her nose. The room pulsed with laughter and loud voices. Several men leaned against the bar, while others stood around the billiard tables watching players line up their shots. All the men, except the bartender, wore hats: bowler hats, flat caps, floppy wide-brimmed hats, and battered felt hats that looked stiff and hard. Most of the men were covered in dust, with drips of candle wax splattered on their boots, pants, and shirts.

Kathy slipped to the corner of the room and sat on the floor, half-hidden by two empty chairs. She hugged her knees close, trying to be as small as possible. Her heart skipped a few beats when she realized David hadn't followed. Tough, she thought, taking a deep breath to gather courage. She lifted her chin and looked about.

The men at the billiard tables placed bets on who would win, commenting on good shots and shaking their heads when the ball missed its mark. Conversations rolled around in the same odd-sounding accent James had. At the other end of the room, tenor and baritone voices swelled up and down as they belted out a song:

The blackbirds and thrushes sang in the green bushes;
The wood doves and larks seem'd to mourn for the maid;
And this song that she sang be concerning her lover:
O, Jimmy will be slain in the wars, I'm afraid.

The singers sloshed their beer, gulped down a swig, then continued with another verse. Kathy almost didn't notice when David walked into the saloon. He slid over to the far billiard table and mingled with the men. He was as tall as most of them. Except for the lack of mustache and candle wax drippings, he could have passed for a young miner. Kathy stared at him, trying to reconcile this image with that of her bossy brother.

Tucking her shoes under her skirt, she scrunched smaller against the wall. Her head ached under the weight of loud voices and the stink of stale beer. The busy pattern of the wallpaper blurred before her eyes as she traced it around the room, sliding past heavy gold-framed pictures and a large gilded mirror. Her eyes had begun to droop when the screech of a chair leg scraping on wood startled her out of her daze. Two men sat in the chairs beside her.

"I tell 'ee, 'e's not found a new vein. 'E said the

knockers be keeping quiet." A man with a bushy beard and crooked pointy nose slapped at his pants, sending dust into Kathy's face. "It don't help none the price of silver be dropping."

The second man leaned back in his chair, his jaw working hard as he chewed on a rather large wad. "If we don't hit new ore soon, this town's going to roll over and die. I've done seen it before. I hear the bosses want to cut our pay, too." The man leaned over and spat at a brass jug on the floor. A gooey brown mass splattered half in the jar and half down its side. Kathy nearly gagged.

"Well, comrade, maybe the knockers will speak to Matthew soon. He's got the knack, 'ee know."

Kathy swiveled on the floor to face the man sitting next to her. "Knockers? Do you mean tommyknockers?"

The pointy-nosed man jumped with a cry, banging the chair against the wall. "What are 'ee doing there, maid? 'Ee startled me awful bad. I didn't see 'ee."

His companion leaned forward to look at Kathy. "What *are* you doing there? This ain't no place for a gal."

Kathy smiled, trying to ignore the brown spittle dripping down the scraggly beard. "I'm waiting for my uncle. He told me to stay here, out of the way. He'll be back soon."

The spittle-face man squinted. "You ain't one of those fancy gals, is you?" He eyed Kathy's soiled dress, dirty face, and wind-bedraggled hair.

The pointy-nosed man smacked his companion on

the arm. "What you be saying, Tom. This 'ere be a young maid, a mere child. Bill don't let no fancy girls in 'ere." He looked down at Kathy. "'E don't let no women in 'ere at all. Child, it ain't fitty and proper for 'ee to be 'ere. Some sorry man 'ee uncle be to leave 'ee 'ere."

Kathy shrugged, unsure how to respond. "What about the knockers? Can anybody hear the tommy-knockers?" She lowered her voice. "Wouldn't that be scary?"

The man cracked a laugh. "Not for Matthew. Knockers talk to Matthew free-like. Matthew, 'e told the captain where the last silver vein be, and thicky vein be right where he said it be. Course, some say it be luck. Matthew, now, 'e says 'twas the knockers."

Kathy jumped as the sharp shrill of a whistle cut through the howl of the wind.

"Time to go," the pointy-nosed man said. He rose and stretched his legs. "Don't 'ee stay 'ere long," he said to Kathy as his companion stood and spat one last time toward the brass jug. Together, the two men walked out the saloon door.

David edged around the billiard tables and made his way toward Kathy. "Come on," he said, reaching for her hand. "We've got to get to the barn."

Kathy tucked her hand behind her. "But he's here."

"The Nose?"

"No, the gifted one."

"In the saloon?"

"No, not here. In town. They were talking about him."

"We'll find him tomorrow. We've got to go. Frank and James are waiting. We need those blankets."

Kathy glanced around the saloon, trying to hear other conversations. "But I didn't get his last name. I still don't know where to find him. I've got to stay."

"No," David said. He grabbed her arm and hauled her to her feet. Several men turned their way and scowled. "Come on," David grumbled under his breath. "You're not supposed to be here, anyway." More faces turned their way. Aware of the unfriendly glances, Kathy trudged behind David and out the saloon door.

"David, listen to me," she said, tugging at his sleeve. He couldn't hear her. The wind roared too loudly in their ears. The gale snatched David's hat and whipped it down the street, forcing the two to chase after it. Shoved by a windy fist, they flew down the street. As they passed the second saloon, a bareheaded Frank darted out to join them. He waved for them to stop.

"I found it. I found it," he shouted, trying to be heard over the blustery howl.

"Found what?" David yelled back.

"The No Name. I found the No Name mine!"

14 Diphtheria

Frank hollered something else, but Kathy couldn't hear. David shook his head and pointed toward the barn. Together, they ran down the street, the wind flinging them along. Laughing, Frank and David flapped their arms like a pair of geese while Kathy stumbled along behind. She rounded the corner of the barn and ran smack into James, who held her up so she wouldn't fall.

"You be in Caribou now, where the wind be born," he shouted over the noise, coughing as the cold caught his throat.

David let out a whoop and held his side to catch his breath. "I'm glad we don't have to walk against this." A sudden look of dismay spread over his face. "Or do we?"

James chuckled, pulling his cap down farther on his head and drawing his oversized coat close around him. "Every bloody step."

"Every bloody step is right," Kathy muttered as she practically crawled up the slope on hands and knees. The wind buffeted her from the side, making it impossible to stand. It whipped her hair into her face so she could barely see.

She followed the dark shadow that was James to the edge of town, where he stopped to rummage inside two miners' shacks. They were both small, one-room structures with bunks built into the corner walls. Rustic, homemade tables, block-wood chairs, and tiny stoves crowded into the remaining space. There was barely enough room left for Kathy and the boys to squeeze into.

At the first shack, Kathy gathered up a blanket and almost added a pillow until she noticed the dark oily spot in the middle of its calico slip. She wrinkled her nose and turned away, deciding her dirty jeans and T-shirt would make a better headrest.

"I hope our shack is in better shape," she said as they left the second cabin and struggled farther up the slope.

It wasn't.

James pointed to a rickety shed perched on the top of the hill. It groaned under the weight of the western wind, threatening to topple over despite two poles propping it up on the east side. "There her be," James said.

The door nearly flew off its hinges as he opened it. Inside, newspapers littered the floor, swirling around in the draft that blew through a large crack in the wall. Debris lay everywhere.

"I'm afraid it be a tad cold," he said. "Frank, 'elp me 'ere with the fire."

They hauled in bits of wood lying scattered around the building. Soon a small fire crackled in the crumbling fireplace, its flames dancing in the draft. The four of them sat on the floor beside the fire and stretched their fingers toward the flames. When their hands felt a little warmer, James reached into a bag slung over his shoulder and pulled out a bundle wrapped in cloth and a round, lidded pot with a single drinking cup, upside down, stuck to its top.

"I told me mum some new mates o' mine be a bit down on food. I didn't say naught else," he quickly added. "She sent 'ee some pasties and a bit o' saffron cake. And 'ere be some tea, too." He handed the package and the pot to Kathy. "Thicky ought to take care of 'ee." He grinned, then turned away to cough. He swallowed hard and grimaced. "Me throat's a bit sore," he said, rubbing his neck. "I got to be going 'ome now. I'll be 'ere in the mornin'." Coughing, he waved goodbye, opened the door, and staggered out into the wind.

Kathy unwrapped the cloth, releasing a savory, steamy smell. Piled inside, she found three large, stuffed mounds of golden-brown pie dough crimped along the edges so they formed half-moons. They were still hot to the touch. Beside them, wrapped in bits of paper, lay three slices of yellow cake. Her stomach growled in anticipation of her first hot meal since Boulder.

"Shall we eat it?" she asked, barely able to take her eyes off the golden pasty.

Frank licked his lips. "We've only got one can of peaches left. We really should wait until tomorrow," he said half-heartedly.

David stared at the pasty. "Maybe if we share just one."

Frank already had his knife halfway out of his pocket. "Sounds good to me."

He took a pasty from Kathy's hand, cut it into three pieces, then passed them around. With mouth watering, Kathy curled her fingers around the warm pie crust and sank her teeth into a delicious mixture of cooked beef, potatoes, and onions. She thought she had never eaten anything so good. She chewed slowly, relishing every bite. When she was done, she licked her fingers, then wiped them on her dress.

"So what about the No Name?" she asked, remembering the riddle now that she felt warmer inside and out.

"Oh, the No Name," Frank said, gulping down a cupful of tea. "It's here—in Caribou. The riddle said, 'up to the No Name he will flee, to seek and steal the missing key.' I thought that old gnome, that tommyknocker, or whatever he is, was being a jerk and wouldn't give us the name of the place. Turns out there's a mine called the No Name." He tossed a piece of wood into the fire, arousing spitting sparks. "Why couldn't he make it clear? I mean, he could have said, 'Go up the canyon to the No Name mine, there the man you'll be sure to find,' or something like that. And why did he mention gold? The No Name is a silver mine. Boy, that old dwarf makes me mad."

Kathy picked up her blanket and pulled it over her shoulders. "Maybe gold means the map. The map's of a gold mine, and The Nose can't use it until he finds the missing piece. So he's still after gold, even if he comes to Caribou."

Frank just shook his head. "Dang old tommy-knocker."

"What's the rest of your riddle, Frank?" David asked. "Are there other clues?"

Frank cleared his throat. "'All script in bronze, he'll find the key, not meant to satisfy man's greed. It opens more than just a map; the Otherworld lies at its lap.' What do you suppose that means, the Otherworld?"

Kathy poked at the fire with a stick. "Do you suppose," she said, "that Mrs. Acheson is right—that there are other worlds besides our own?"

Neither Frank nor David responded, but she caught Frank staring at her with an odd expression on his face. Suddenly ill at ease, she tossed the stick in the fire, and drew her blanket tighter.

"My riddle mentions the key, too," she said. "'So find the man who owns the key, a gifted one who hears and sees.' I think I know who it is. Well, at least I think I know what his first name is—Matthew. We've got to find him. And we've got to find him fast."

"Maybe," David said. Claiming a blanket, he curled up against the wall away from the wind. "But I still want to find The Nose," he added, covering his head.

Feeling dismissed, Kathy plopped her rolled-up jeans and T-shirt on the floor and lay down near the fire. Despite the fire's warmth and her fatigue, she couldn't fall asleep. She tossed and turned on the hard wooden floor as the shack moaned under the unrelenting rush of the wind. Every now and then she heard the scritch-scratch of tiny feet scurrying on the boards. Mice, she thought, until she saw red shiny eyes staring out of the darkness. They were too big for mice. Alarmed, she moved closer to David and Frank, carefully positioning Frank between herself and the place where she had seen the glimmering eyes.

The fire had burned to simmering embers by the time Kathy fell into a fitful sleep. A bony finger jabbed in the air while a laughing, winking face with thick, black bangs said, "It ain't fitty for a woman to be in the bal." Mrs. Acheson swirled round and round stating, "Great-grandfather Penhallow had the gift," while a pointy-nosed face answered back, "Matthew, now, 'e says 'twas the knockers." Whispers echoed back and forth, "To save this man you may be late," until a high, shrill, whistle cut through the air. Kathy woke with a start. The night shift was over.

She pushed back damp strands of hair, and pulled the blanket closer to shut out the cold mountain air. She felt unsettled, worried, without knowing why. Perhaps it was the stillness of the morning after the rattling of the wind last night. To ease her nerves, she stretched out her leg and prodded a formless bundle of blanket with her foot.

"You guys awake?"

A groan escaped from the pile. "I don't think I ever went to sleep," Frank's muffled voice grumbled from under the covers. "I saw rats last night." He threw back the blanket and grabbed the wool coat he had dumped on the floor. "A hot shower would be nice."

"David?" Kathy called.

A hand protruded from the other blanket. The blanket rose up and David's head popped out. "A decent bed would be nice, too," he added, running his fingers through his dirty hair.

Kathy pushed her blanket off and folded it into a neat square. "Hurry up. James will be here soon, and we have to get these blankets back before the miners return."

Grumbling, the boys plopped their blankets on top of Kathy's, then sat sullenly by the fire. Frank poked at the dying embers and added fresh kindling on top. The tinder-dry wood exploded into flames, causing David to jump.

"That was stupid!"

"Oh, yeah?"

Angry words were exchanged back and forth. Hoping to cheer everyone up, Kathy opened the package of pasties and cake and passed them around. Eating in silence, they finished the meat pies and swallowed the cake despite its odd, bitter taste. Then one by one, they filed out the door and sat on the ground to wait.

The bright sun felt deliciously warm on Kathy's face in the crisp mountain air, melting away her nagging unease. Around her, pink, blue, and yellow wildflowers bobbed their heads in a breeze that blew the town's rank odor away from the shack. She breathed deeply, enjoying the scent of pine that mingled in the air, just as it did in Boulder Canyon. If they could just clean up the garbage, she thought, Caribou would be a nice place to live. Maybe.

She glanced at the shaft-houses crowding the western slope with their massive piles of discarded rock. To the south and east of Caribou additional mines dotted the hillsides, and a large structure to the south reminded Kathy of the mill in Nederland. She stared at the mines, watching the small figures of men moving in and out of the buildings, sometimes hauling wood in from large stacked piles, but usually hauling rock out. She didn't know what to think of the man-made holes in the earth, except she didn't want to go near them.

"Where is he?" Kathy said, rising to pace back and forth along the front of the cabin. "The miners have got to be home by now." She scanned the hill, straining to see any sign of the skinny boy. As the minutes ticked by, her sense of unease returned. They were losing time. "We can't wait all day," she said. "We've got to find the gifted one. We've got to find Matthew."

David quit examining a rock in his hand, and pitched it down the hill. "You don't know it's some guy named Matthew," he said. "And there could be lots of Matthews. I say we find The Nose and follow him, just like the riddle said."

Frank stood up and brushed off his pants. "Forget The Nose. We're supposed to find the key."

"What do you know?" David snapped.

"I found the mine, didn't I?" Frank shot back, his face flushed with anger.

"Stop it," Kathy said. "We've got to find Matthew. We've got to. . . ." She stopped mid-sentence as pieces of her dream fit snuggly into place. "It's Matthew Penhallow," she said. "It's Mrs. Acheson's great-grand-father." Two blank faces blinked at her.

"I don't know—"

David stopped talking as the soft murmur of voices floated up over the hill. A long line of men, women, and children slowly climbed the winding road up the mountain.

"Quick," Frank cried. "Hide." He grabbed David and Kathy and pulled them behind the cabin. But the voices didn't sound quite right. They almost sounded like weeping.

Kathy stuck her head around the corner. Puzzled, she watched the procession meander up the hill, following the road west toward a large clump of trees. Several men carried a small box on their shoulders. The case was no longer than a yardstick.

"What is it?" Kathy asked, stepping into the open.

Frank frowned. "It looks like a funeral," he said as he stood next to her. "That box is awfully small, though."

David edged past his sister and pointed up the hill. "Look! It's a cemetery. Some little kid must have died."

Drawn toward the solemn, weeping line, Kathy drifted forward. She followed the procession to the clump of trees where marble headstones stuck out of the ground along with wooden crosses. In a few places, torn and broken soil revealed the site of freshly dug graves still waiting for a memorial marker. The smallest was only a few feet long.

The procession stopped and formed a loosely knit circle in a quiet, shady spot as people waited for stragglers to finish climbing the hill. Underneath trees twisted

and bent as if burdened with grief, a small hole in the ground lay next to two other recently dug graves.

"Look," Frank whispered behind Kathy. He pointed to a girl, no older than eight, who stood on the outer edge of the trees. She seemed more an observer than a participant as her hands fiddled nervously with the worn smock that covered her dark dress. "That's James's sister. We can ask her where James is."

Kathy hesitated until David strolled up carrying their clothes and the remaining can of peaches. Then, she nodded at Frank. Anything was better than waiting.

Sister and brother followed Frank over to the cemetery. He slid up beside the small, black-haired girl and touched her gently on the hand. Large expressive eyes, brimming with tears, looked back. Kathy stared in wonder at the child—a black-haired beauty, her dad would have said. James's voice drifted into her mind, "Frank 'ere said you'm be as purty as my sister." She felt herself turn red.

"Mary Beth," Frank said, "remember me? I'm Frank. I'm looking for James. Do you know where he is?"

Mary Beth's lip trembled as tears rolled down her face. "'E's sick, 'e is. Got the diphtheria. I don't want he to die."

"Aw," Frank said, patting the girl's shoulder. "He'll be just fine. He just had a cough, that's all."

"No," the girl said, gathering her smock into a tight ball. "'Ee don't understand. 'E's got the diphtheria. Just like Anna and Willie, and now little Alice Mae." Mary Beth waved at the two new graves and the little coffin resting on the ground. "Anna, her be my friend," she whispered. She turned. At the sight of Kathy, her eyes popped wide and her mouth dropped. "'Tis that 'ee cousin? The one with the red 'air?" She clapped her hands over her mouth. "'Tis an omen," she cried. "A death omen." Sobbing, she fled down the hill.

Kathy felt her heart skip a beat. "What did she mean—a death omen?" she whispered.

A short, pale-faced man with sympathetic eyes walked over and patted her on the back. "Don't worry none. The girl didn't mean no 'arm. 'Tis a tale from the old country, 'tis. Mostly it comes to naught." He watched quietly as two men lowered the coffin into its grave. A white cross of daisies fluttered on top until it too disappeared into the earth. "It be a sorry time when a family loses a child. The Richards now have lost three. Diphtheria be calling too many to the Lord." He shook his head and mumbled as he walked away. "We've got to clean up this town."

The garbage, Kathy thought. Could it be the garbage? She looked down at her own dirty hands, apron, and dress.

"What's diphtheria?" Frank asked in a half-whisper.

"Never heard of it," David said softly as a man opened a Bible and led the funeral party in prayer. Kathy felt numb. The coffin was so small. So were the other two graves. The children had to have been young. Would another child in the family die? And what about James?

Frank shifted nervously. "Can we get it?" he asked.

David chewed his lip. "I got shots when I was little, but I don't remember what they were for. I've never heard of diphtheria."

The man leading the group closed his Bible as the prayer came to an end. A rich melody of baritones and tenors rose into the air, accompanied by the soft lilt of the women's voices. The same Cornish voices that filled the saloon with raucous song and laughter the night before now wove a melody so sweet and sad it tore at Kathy's heart.

"It kills," she whispered.

"James has it," Frank added so low Kathy almost didn't hear.

The three of them stood silently watching as the first shovels of dirt were cast onto the casket in the ground. David turned toward his sister and squeezed her arm.

"We've got to get home," he said.

"Like now," Frank added.

15 The Gifted One

W hat does your riddle say, Kath?" David asked as the funeral party made its way back down the mountain. Only two men with shovels remained. "Does it tell how to get home?"

"Not really," Kathy replied glumly, forcing her eyes away from the forlorn grave. "We find the gifted one. We save the key, whatever that is, and . . . 'bring it forth through time and space'—but the riddle doesn't say how."

David grunted and stomped on a rock in the ground. "This is crazy. We'll—" Angry shouts cut him off. Agitated men stood outside the abandoned shack, waving the borrowed blankets and the empty tin pot in the air.

"Uh, oh," Frank said. "Somebody spilled the beans. We better get out of here fast. Come on. I know a place where we can hide."

Leading the way, he darted behind rocks and trees to avoid the angry miners, then ran down the slope toward town. He slowed as they passed a group of laughing children playing tag with several barking dogs. Kathy stopped a moment to catch her breath, feeling safer in the company of other kids. Blending in was a good way to hide. But Frank kept going.

"Not far," he said, as he hurried up the hill on the west side of town. He slipped around a ramshackle house and jumped into a small ravine that sprouted out of the mountain slope and spilled into the valley below. At the mouth of the ravine, a large hole yawned in the side of the mountain with water dribbling out through its rocky teeth.

"In here," Frank said as he climbed inside. "It's an abandoned mine, I think. I found it yesterday. We can hide here while we figure out what to do."

Following Frank, Kathy slid into the ravine and scrambled through the gaping hole, ducking below the large slab of rock that braced the mountain above. The cave dipped down, then opened up, allowing her to stand by a pool of water. Frank beckoned for her to follow deeper into the mountain, past the dwindling light and into the dark.

"No way," she said, dropping her bundle of clothes on a sandy spot, still lit by the outside sun. "This is as far as I go."

"It's flat here anyway," David said, bringing up the rear. He tossed his bundle next to hers. Reluctantly, Frank crept back, stooping to avoid hitting his head on the rocks above.

"Fine," he said, dropping his clothes next to theirs. "Now what?"

"We need to find The Nose," David said. "We're supposed to follow him. He's the way home. I just know it."

"Forget The Nose," Frank argued, kicking at a rock. "It's the key we need. We've got to find the key. 'It opens more than just a map.' It's got to be the way home."

"No," Kathy protested. "We've got to find Matthew. He's in danger. 'To save this man you may be late.' Isn't that more important?" Her stomach tightened with a growing sense of urgency bordering on fear. Was it already too late? Would they find him in time? She wanted desperately to go home, but she wanted to save Matthew more. Maybe he also heard whispers in the dark.

They argued back and forth until at last they decided David would look for The Nose, while Frank would help Kathy find Matthew.

"After all," Frank said, "if we find the gifted one, we find the key."

Together, they crawled out into the sunshine. Without looking back, David charged down the hill toward town. Frank and Kathy decided to head for the nearest shaft-house, instead.

The first mine was a flop. When they asked for Matthew, the men shooed them away as they eyed Kathy's red hair. The second and third weren't much better. The miners either shook their heads or scolded them. "Don't you know the mines aren't safe? Get home with you, now."

Finally, Kathy and Frank gave up and traipsed up and down the town streets, asking about Matthew. A few shop owners recognized the name, but knew only that he worked at the mines. Others merely shook their heads. Finally, the man at Murphy's Meat Market directed them to a small house up on the far hill.

It perched alone on the mountainside, away from the ripple of laughing children and the hubbub of town. The heavy quiet felt almost unnatural. Timidly, Kathy tapped on the door, then she followed with a louder rap. No one answered.

"Maybe he's working," Frank offered, pressing his face against a darkened window to look inside.

"Figures," Kathy said, plopping down on the front steps. She scooted over into a shady spot, seeking relief from the burning sun that defied yesterday's cold.

"Maybe we should go inside," Frank said, testing the door handle.

"No. We wait. We don't want him to be mad."

"Oh, all right." Frank picked up a piece of kindling from the pile stacked against the house and sat on the ground. He pulled out his pocketknife and sliced at the wood.

Bored and tired, Kathy tossed pebbles at a dead tree stump until she remembered the paper in her pocket and the broken pencil from the Brainard Hotel. She pulled out the pencil and one clean sheet of paper to draw on.

A large tree grew out of the lines on the page, a tree with sweeping branches that curled at the top and dipped down toward the ground. Tangled roots turned and twisted in the dirt below until they stretched up to kiss the air. Limbs and roots almost touched, like two hands outstretched but not quite clasping.

"Cool," Frank said, looking over her shoulder.

Kathy glanced at the carving in his hand and raised her eyebrows in surprise. "Where did you learn to do that?" she asked, pointing to the crude figure of an owl.

Frank opened his mouth to reply, but closed it again as a short man with stooped shoulders limped toward them, carrying a brown package stuffed under the sleeve of his tattered, clay-stained coat. A thick black mustache twitched against a pale, square face as he squinted at Kathy and Frank with emerald-green eyes.

"What 'ave us 'ere?" he asked. "Two that belong in school, I'm sure."

Kathy stood up and dusted off the back of her dress.

"Are you Matthew Penhallow?" she asked. She already knew the answer. She had seen those eyes before.

"Aas, I be Matthew," he said with a nod. He tilted his head and waited.

Now that she had found him, Kathy didn't know what to ask. Frank didn't seem to know, either.

"Speak on, child," Matthew said, shifting the package in his arms.

"Do you hear tommyknockers?" Kathy finally blurted, feeling terribly foolish.

Matthew chuckled. "You'm thinking about the knockers, you?" He scraped his wax-spattered work boots on a nearby stump, then reached for the door and pushed. "Come in and I'll tell 'ee what 'ee want to know."

He stepped inside the house and glanced around the front room that served as both kitchen and parlor.

"It's some quiet 'ere without my Clara and the children. They'm in Boulder now. It weren't safe 'ere with all the diphtheria." He placed the brown package on the kitchen table and eased himself into a cane-bottomed chair, careful not to put too much weight on his right foot. He removed his bowler hat from his head and placed it on the table. "Now, what be it 'ee want to know, you?"

"Do you hear—?"

"The key," Frank interrupted. "Do you have a key?"

"A key?" Matthew replied. "I don't need no key, my son. The door's not locked."

Frank shook his head. "No, I mean—I don't know what I mean. 'All script in bronze he'll find the key.'"

"Bronze? 'Ee mean me pendant?" From under his thick flannel shirt, he pulled out a bronze medallion that hung on a chain around his neck. On the outer edges, an intricate pattern of knots twisted and turned among themselves. In the center, a tree stood with boughs that intertwined and curled around toward the bottom, to become the tree's roots, creating a continuous circle of interlacing limbs. Engraved in the trunk were three birds, forming a triangle.

"Kathy, it's your tree," Frank said. "How on earth did you know?"

Kathy stared at the medallion in shock.

"'Tis the tree of life," Matthew said, fingering the pendant. "It connects the three worlds with its limbs."

"What three worlds?" Kathy whispered not taking her eyes off the pendant.

"In the old faith, there be three worlds—the Gods above, the Earth, and the spirits below. Some say there be more to this world than what most men see." Matthew's eyes sparkled as he watched Kathy's and Frank's faces.

"Spirits?" Frank said. "You mean—ghosts?"

"Aas," Matthew replied. "Other spirits, too," he added with a smile. "'Ave 'ee not heard them at night or felt their breath?"

Kathy could feel blood drain from her face. She could barely breathe. Her parents had always assured her that the noises in the dark or the shivers in her spine were nothing but an overactive imagination. Now she knew they were real.

"Why are those birds there?" Frank asked, pointing to the images on the tree's trunk. Kathy wondered if Frank knew what Matthew had really said.

"Thicky be the eagle, the owl, and the blackbird," Matthew replied, pointing to each bird in turn. "In the old faith, they be the three elders of the world. The eagle, 'e be strong and fierce and flies high into the sky. 'E's a wise old messenger between Earth and the world above. The owl 'ere be a bird of the night, keeping company with creatures of the dark and the world below. The black-bird, now, 'e sings the way between the worlds, easing the journey through in-between places. The three elders. They speak of sky and darkness and shimmering time."

Kathy stared at the pendant, then took a tentative step forward. "Do you—do you hear them?" she asked. "Do you hear whispers in the dark?"

Matthew gazed out the window with unseeing eyes. "Aas," he replied softly. "All the time." He smiled at Kathy. "It's me heritage. That's why I bear this 'ere pendant. It be a sign given to me family by the Otherworld long ago to mark our line. Other families bear it, too. It opens the doors from one world to the next."

"'It opens more than just a map,'" Frank whispered as his fingers stretched out for the medallion. "'The Otherworld lies at its lap.'"

"What do 'ee know about a map?" Matthew barked, shoving Frank's hand away from the pendant and seizing his arm.

"N—Nothing," Frank stammered as he struggled to escape Matthew's grip. With a jerk, Frank twisted his arm loose from Matthew's hand, tearing the sleeve on his coat. He stumbled backward, and nearly fell. Matthew pushed himself up out of the chair.

"John said some cobba stole 'is map. Said it might be a boy, tall boy like 'ee." Matthew glared at Frank. "How do 'ee know about the map? 'Ave 'ee come to steal me pendant?" Knocking over the chair, he snatched at Frank. Frank twisted to the right and dodged out of the way.

"Come on," he shouted, pulling Kathy out the door. "Run."

Stunned and frightened, Kathy did exactly as he said. They raced through town, slipping between buildings to hide. Matthew couldn't run fast with his limp—but he certainly could blast out a yell. Soon half the town was in an uproar.

Frantically, Kathy and Frank slipped behind the weathered house by the cave and scrambled into the ditch, hoping no one saw them. Kathy gasped for air as she staggered back into the quiet of the mountain.

"What were you thinking?" she asked, fighting back tears. "The whole town is after us now. And what about the whispers?" She sat on a rock and began to cry.

"What whispers?" Frank asked, then lowered his voice. "You really hear them, don't you?" Kathy didn't bother to nod. She hugged her chest and closed her eyes. How would they get home now?

Frank stuck his hands in his pockets and awkwardly shuffled from one foot to the next. "It's okay," he said. "It'll be all right. Hey," he added brightly. "I'll go get some firewood." He poked Kathy in the arm. "Maybe we'll have steak tonight."

Kathy almost laughed despite her misery. Frank grinned at her smile and disappeared outside.

As the day wore on, they waited for David at the mouth of the cave. Frank found another piece of wood and pulled out his knife to whittle, while Kathy sat quietly for a long time, lost in thought. She kept thinking about Matthew, the riddle, and the creature under the porch. Finally, she took the last piece of clean paper out of her pocket and began to sketch, careful to draw flowers this time.

Hours crept by. Long shadows stretched down the slope as the sun dipped below the mountain to the west. Still no David.

"I'll go build a fire," Frank said, putting away his

knife and carving. He ducked into the cave, leaving Kathy to keep watch. She stared out into the dusk as it settled over the land and deepened into night, igniting twinkling lights in the houses and saloons below.

"Where is he, Frank?" she asked as she left her perch and knelt by the fire. "What if something's wrong? Maybe we should look for him."

"Where?" Frank replied. "He could be anywhere." He stirred black ashes into the dirt, then sighed. "Maybe we should eat," he said, picking up the last can of peaches.

He cut open the lid, scooped out some peaches, then passed the fruit to Kathy. They ate two-thirds of the food, leaving the rest for David, then settled into a comfortable silence as the firelight flickered on the rocky walls.

The silence didn't last for long. A siren shrieked through the cold night air and bounced off the surrounding rock. Kathy jumped and twisted around. Now, she *was* scared. Not of the dark. Not of the voices. She was afraid for David. Night shift had started and he still wasn't back.

"Frank, I—" A clattering noise interrupted her.

"I found him," David gasped, as he slid over the lip of the ravine and into the cave. "I found The Nose! I think there's going to be trouble. He just followed some guy named Matthew into the No Name mine."

16 The Black Hole

It took several moments for Kathy and Frank to absorb what David had said, moments filled with stunned silence before they blurted out their questions.

"What do you mean some guy named Matthew?"

"What do you mean the No Name mine?"

Kathy felt sick. The three riddles had crossed, coming together. David was right. There was going to be trouble.

"Are you sure it was Matthew?" she asked.

"Are you sure it was the No Name?" Frank said.

David bent over to cough before nodding. "I saw the sign on the building. It was the No Name, all right. And as for the guy, one of the miners greeted him, calling him by name and asking about his foot. A rock fell on it or something." David sat on a boulder and coughed again.

Kathy frowned at her brother's pale face. Tiny beads of sweat glistened in the flickering light. "Are you all right?" she asked. "Are you getting sick?"

"No," he said, wiping his face with his sleeve. "I'm just out of breath."

She looked over at Frank, fearful that David was wrong. Her brother was the best player on his soccer team. He never was out of breath.

"It's the altitude," Frank said, meeting Kathy's eye. "He's not used to it. It gives folks a headache, too." He picked up the leftover peaches and handed them to David. "Here, have something to eat. It'll make you feel better. Then tell us everything that happened."

David took the can and stuffed a peach into his mouth. "I found The Nose at the hotel," he said between bites, "and followed him all afternoon. He spent most of the day in the bar. He asked a lot of questions. How did the miners find new veins? Who was good at it? How long did the night shift last? How deep were the mines? But then his questions got weird. Did accidents happen very often? What caused them? Were there ever any fights? He made a bunch of miners real unhappy. They didn't like his questions. Said they would bring bad luck. The miners were real glad when The Nose got up to leave. I thought he'd go back to the hotel. He didn't. Instead, he followed a guy with a limp."

"Matthew Penhallow," Frank said.

David nodded. "The Nose followed Matthew up to the No Name mine. He tried to go down the shaft with him but the foreman stopped him—said he didn't belong and should leave. The Nose didn't. He hung around outside until the coast was clear. Then he crept back in, climbed into the shaft bucket, and rang the signal bell. Last I saw him, he was going down the mine-shaft in the bucket."

Kathy groaned. "The Nose is after the key. It's a pendant, David, around Matthew's neck. I've been thinking about it. The map had instructions to the lost vein of gold, something about a blackbird and an owl. The pendant has both. It's the missing piece to the map."

"'Incomplete the map he'll find, and so he'll plan a blacker crime.' Something's going to happen. Something bad."

David put into words what Kathy already knew. Time *was* running out. She could feel it. And she was the only one who could fix it. She closed her eyes, trying to calm her inner turmoil, but it didn't work. She opened her eyes and took a deep breath.

"I have to go after them. I have to save the key."

"No way," David said.

"Forget it," Frank added.

"I have to," she said. "'It is the key that you must save, don't let me take it to its grave.' I have to save the key. And . . . I think the mine is the grave." She shuddered. "I hate dark places. And holes in the ground."

"But Kath," David said, "you'd have to go down in a creaky bucket. It's dangerous. You might . . . I mean . . . I'll go. I'll go find them. I'm stronger. It'll be safer for me." He stood up, sucked in his breath, and wiggled his arms and hands to loosen them up. But he couldn't erase the fear on his face.

"You can't," Kathy said. "Didn't you listen? 'Don't let *me* take it to its grave.' 'Me,' David. That means the dwarf under the porch. He's involved somehow. You said yourself that this was my fault. If it weren't for me, we wouldn't see him, we wouldn't hear him, we wouldn't be here. And," she said, looking her brother in the eye, "I think you're right. I hear things. I feel things. Just like Matthew said. Somehow I did this and somehow I have to fix it. I have to go down—alone."

David opened his mouth to protest, then looked away as conflicting emotions flickered across his face. "I didn't mean it," he finally whispered.

"Yes, you did," Kathy said. "And it's okay. Someday, you'll have to tell me about Grandma Faye." She fingered her once-silky strands of hair, now stiff from dirt and wind. "Cut it," she said, turning toward Frank.

"Wh—what?" he stammered, shock and surprise rippling over his face.

"Cut it," she repeated. "The miners will never let me near the mine as a 'red-haired maid.'"

Frank pushed her hand away from her hair. "No, you don't want to do that. I was just kidding before in Boulder. Well, sort of. But—"

"Cut it," Kathy commanded. "We don't have time to argue. Matthew is in danger and I have to save the key. If I don't, we'll never get home. Just do it." Kathy never felt so sure of anything in her life. For the first time since she left her house at midnight, she knew exactly what she had to do—no matter how scared she was.

She sat in the light of the fire, turning her back to Frank. She heard the click of the knife as it opened and felt its tug on her hair. Frank sawed at the strands while David held them away from her skin.

"We'll try not to make it look *too* bad," David said, grimacing as Frank slashed. "It'll grow back."

Kathy didn't want to know. She closed her eyes and thought about Matthew. "Done," Frank said, as he took one last slice.

Kathy ran her fingers over her chopped hair and bit her lip, trying not to show the pain she felt inside. Frank had cut it short around her ears but a little longer in the back. It felt uneven, unkempt. It would have to do.

She shooed the boys out of the cave while she changed from her dress into jeans, T-shirt, and jacket. Cotton and denim had never felt so good. Almost as an afterthought, she reached into the pocket of her discarded apron and pulled out Rocky Mountain Joe's picture of an owl. She slipped it into her jacket pocket. If she had to go into darkness, maybe, just maybe, she could remember the wonders of the night.

She called Frank and David back.

Frank unrolled his nylon jacket and pulled out a familiar cap. He placed it on Kathy's head.

"There," he said, adjusting the hat so it didn't fall over her eyes. "That'll make you look more like a boy. James left it last night. I was going to give it back this morning."

Kathy smiled, trying not to show how shaky she felt. "So," she said. "Where's the No Name?"

Together they walked to the mine, Frank leading the way while David stayed close by Kathy's side. They followed the road up the hill to the west, where massive mounds of waste rock littered the hillside. Above each mound, a large shaft-house perched, its tall iron pillars puffing smoke into the night. There were so many shaft-houses on the hill that Kathy imagined a beehive of tunnels in the rock below. She wondered if they were walking above one now and shivered at the thought of the earth collapsing beneath her.

The shaft-house to the No Name mine was small compared to others. Still, it sprawled like a warehouse across the hill, sheltering equipment, working men, and, most importantly, the mineshaft itself. A low rumble throbbed in the air as the trio approached the door. David pulled Kathy to a halt.

"I followed The Nose when he crept back inside," he said. "The mineshaft is a hole in the floor at the back wall. There's a bunch of men sorting rock on the main floor. You'll have to avoid them, but they're pretty busy checking the stone for silver and gold. They don't look up very often."

Kathy nodded with understanding. "How do I get down?"

"You'll have to go down in the bucket like The Nose. Either that or climb down the ladder on the side of the shaft. It's a really deep hole and if you slipped. . . . It's too dangerous, Kath. You know how you . . . well . . . just take the bucket."

He squeezed her arm. "They've got a bell system. I think it's posted by the shaft, but The Nose, he just rang the bell twice. Seemed to work. Anyway, they lowered the bucket. And don't forget candles," he continued. "They've got this box of candles on the floor near the shaft. All the miners took three or four before they went down into the hole."

Frank grabbed Kathy's other arm. "Here," he said digging into his pockets. "Take these." He handed her his book of matches.

She stared at the matches, jarred by the solid touch in her hand. This was real. She was going into a mine, into the darkness of her worst nightmare. She looked up at her brother, trying to swallow her fear.

David punched her lightly on the arm. "You can do it," he said. "But you still don't *have* to."

Tears filled her eyes as she shoved the matches into her jeans pocket.

"Yes, I do," she said. Squaring her shoulders, she took a deep breath, then walked through the door.

She found herself in a large open room littered with

piles of rock and unfamiliar equipment. At the far end, three men chatted through the clatter of rock as they sorted the stone in the dingy light cast by kerosene lamps. Kathy sidled against the wall, trying to stay in the shadows. She moved carefully toward the back of the room, grateful for the quiet rubber of her tennis shoes and the loud roar of the boiler as it hungrily consumed wood in the small engine room nearby. But where was the shaft?

Looking for a clue, she glanced at the steel cable, pipes, and tubes overhead that snaked out of the engine room. They drooped and draped their way to the back of the room. There the pipes and tubes dropped directly to the floor while the cable curled over a large wheel on top of a tall tower, before it, too, slunk down to a hole in the floor. That was it—the mineshaft!

The shaft was split into two compartments, neatly framed with large beams of wood. Down one, the tubes and pipes slipped into the inky darkness, with a hiss of air going down and a gurgle of water coming up. Beside them, the upper handles of a rough wooden ladder stuck up. Above the second compartment, a large cast-iron bucket hung at the end of the cable, its bottom hidden just below floor level. The bucket was huge, reaching as high as Kathy's chest and yawning more than two feet wide at its lip. It could easily hold one man, or a twelve-year-old girl.

She inched over to the hole and peered down. Cold,

damp air flowed out of the mine as if it were a living creature expelling breath. The flux brushed her face and sucked away her air. Terrified, she scrambled back.

"You, there," shouted a man from the sorting floor. "What are you doing? Get away from that shaft. You want to get yourself killed?" He put down the rock in his hand and stood up.

Kathy blinked, but stayed crouched on the floor. She was too scared to move. To her relief, Frank and David charged into the room and strode up to the ore sorter.

"We're looking for work," David said. His voice echoed against the walls, breathless and excited, but controlled. "Could you tell us about jobs?"

Frank picked up a large rock. "Hey, does this have silver in it? How do you tell if it has silver in it? Would it make a good antique?"

All three ore sorters gaped at the two boys, David all businesslike and Frank hopping around like a demented monkey from one pile of stone to the next, picking up rocks and jabbering. No one watched Kathy. It was now or never.

Riding the wave of momentary courage, she pushed herself off the floor, snatched three candles from a box near the shaft, and jammed them in her denim jacket. Mumbling a prayer under her breath, she stepped on a large empty crate and reached for the cable that held the bucket by its massive handle. She placed one foot on the bucket's rim, causing it to sway. Beneath her a black hole gaped open, threatening to suck her in. She merely had to slip.

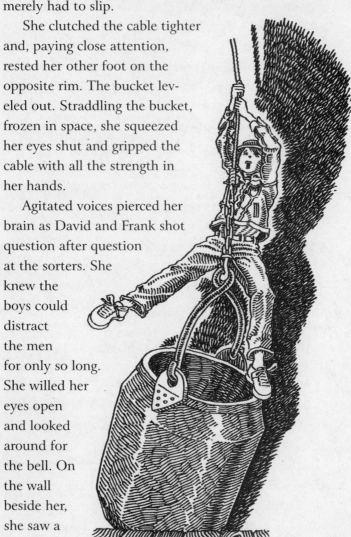

She clutched the cable tighter and, paying close attention, rested her other foot on the opposite rim. The bucket leveled out. Straddling the bucket, frozen in space, she squeezed her eyes shut and gripped the cable with all the strength in her hands.

Agitated voices pierced her brain as David and Frank shot question after question at the sorters. She knew the boys could distract the men for only so long. She willed her eyes open and looked around for the bell. On the wall beside her, she saw a

200

wire hanging down beside a chart. Reluctant to let go of the cable, she carefully reached out with one hand and pulled the wire twice, the sharp ping of a bell ringing each time. Then, grasping the cable tightly with both hands, she slipped her feet inside the bucket's rim. With one final prayer, she let go. She landed with a thud inside the bucket just as it swayed and dropped. Unable to hold back a strangled cry, she plunged down into darkness.

17 Whispers

The bucket spun this way and that as it cracked against the granite wall of the shaft, sending splintered rock rattling into the depths, while the sound of hissing air and gurgling water filled the cold damp stench of water-soaked soil, stone, and timber. Kathy felt sick. She cringed at the bottom of the bucket, scraping its sides with her fingers.

Down she plummeted. Down into blackness so thick it snuffed out even the memory of color and light. Kathy was blind—and she was falling.

She closed her eyes and pressed her hands hard into the jagged bits of rock that littered the bucket's iron floor. Occasionally, shadows of light flitted across her eyelids, then disappeared, until at last the bucket lurched to a stop.

"What's going on?" an angry voice rumbled. "I didn't ask for no bucket."

Kathy opened her eyes, blinking at the light that now bathed the shaft walls in soft, fluttery shadows.

Struggling to see after total darkness, she scrunched deeper into the bucket as footsteps thumped toward her.

"Henry," a muffled voice called from a distance. "Give me a hand, will ya?"

The footsteps stopped, then turned away. Slowly, Kathy pushed herself up to peep over the bucket's rim. Before her, a wide cavity opened in the mountain, lit by candles clinging to the walls. At the rear of the small cavern, a narrow tunnel bored into the rock. A man with rolled-up shirt sleeves and wax-spattered pants took off his stiff felt cap. He lit a candle clasped to its front, then put the hat back on. Picking up a shovel, he clumped down the long, dark tunnel, the pale light from his candle bobbing before him.

Staying low, Kathy scanned the cavern to make sure she was alone. Then she stood, holding the rim on both sides. Careful not to get too close to the bucket's edge, she stretched her neck to peek over at the black chasm below. She was not at the bottom of the mine. Instead, the bucket swung in the middle of what seemed like a bottomless pit. Flat, solid ground beckoned only a hop away. But if she missed. . . . Kathy didn't want to think about that.

Wishing she was more like David, she reached up and grabbed the cable above. She tugged and pulled with all her might, scraping the bucket's sides with her feet in order to push herself up. The bucket swayed with each push and pull, swinging like a wayward pendulum. The sway got wider and wider, throwing Kathy off balance. She thought she was going to drop, when at last one foot snagged the bucket's rim. The other quickly followed. Kathy steadied herself on the bucket's lip, both feet firmly planted, then eyed the jump she'd have to make in order to reach solid ground. It wasn't far. But then, neither was the ditch.

Gathering her courage, she focused on her hands and feet. Then, gritting her teeth, she leaped to the cavity's stone floor. Landing on all fours, she scrambled away from the shaft and pressed herself against the jagged wall. She was in the belly of the earth, with a mountain overhead, but at least there was dirt beneath her feet.

There wasn't much to see at the mouth of the tunnel. Close to the shaft, a cart filled with crumbled stone rested on a metal sheet that spread over the floor. As if emerging from its place of birth, a two-rail track snaked away from the metal sheet and disappeared into the dark interior of the mine, while two shovels leaned against the wall, momentarily at rest. Kathy stared at the track and wondered how to find Matthew. She didn't know where to start and she dared not ask.

"I can't figure it out," a muffled voice said from the depths of the tunnel. A faint light danced in the distance. "They keep sending the bucket down when I don't ask for it. First time, I had to send it back empty. At least this time, I got rock to load."

Kathy cringed at the thought of rock crashing into the bucket. If she had still been there. . . . There were more dangers to a mine than falling.

She scanned the cavern for a place to hide. A short distance down the tunnel, an empty cart stood next to the wall, half-hidden in shadow. She ran to its side and squeezed behind it. Crouching down, she held her breath as the voices and footsteps approached. Two men trudged by. Putting their shovels down by the rock-filled cart, they grabbed its sides. Pushing and pulling it across the metal sheet, they maneuvered the cart close to the shaft where the bucket hung. While their backs were turned, Kathy slipped from her hiding place and darted down the tunnel.

She felt her way in the dark, scraping hands and fingers on ragged rock while stubbing toes on the uneven floor. She thought about her candles, but didn't dare stop, not yet. She crept forward, one shuffle at a time, inhaling damp, dusty air that tasted acrid on her tongue. Behind her, the men's deep voices slowly flattened out and faded as the mountain swallowed them up.

A heavy stillness settled around her as she inched along. It was as if the mountain waited and watched. At last a faint *thud, thud* filtered from the darkness ahead. Kathy reached for a candle and the book of matches. Fingers gently probing shape and form, she pulled out a single match and lit it.

"A woman! A woman! A woman in the mine!" The

words rattled along the craggy walls like pebbles rolling down a rocky slope.

Startled, Kathy dropped the match and stared in horror as it sizzled out. A tingle prickled along her skin. With a sense of panic, she fumbled for another match, nearly dropping the packet from her trembling fingers.

"Who is she?" fluttered in the air, brushing her hair like a whispered breeze.

"Stop it," Kathy cried at the darkness. With a *sphfit,* she struck the second match. "You're scaring me."

"She hears, she hears. The gift. The gift. The woman has the gift."

Steadying the match in her hand, she lit the candle, held it high, and stared wildly about. "Where are you?" Silence replied. She saw nothing but rock and shadow. She turned toward the thudding and ran.

She only ran a short distance before she stumbled and slowed to a walk. The uneven ground threatened to trip her with its litter of rock, wood, and debris. The candlelight didn't help. It cast an eerie glow, fooling eyes, as it slunk in and around corners and rocky protrusions. She kept walking.

Soon the *thud, thud* turned into the *ping, ping* of metal striking metal. Afraid of what she might find, Kathy slowed to a crawl and blew out her flame. She felt her way along the last stretch of rock until she rounded a bend and stopped. At the end of the tunnel, two miners pounded a metal drill into the granite wall, their heavy hammers slamming the drill-head in a fast, steady rhythm. A third man held the metal spike with his hand, turning it in its hole between strikes. Kathy sucked in her breath and dared not speak—one false swing of the hammer and the drill man's hand would be crushed. Soundlessly, she watched while, under the thundering blows, the drill slipped into the solid rock like a pin pressed into clay.

Kathy tried not to cough, but the dusty air caught in her throat. The hammers stopped in mid-swing. Three startled faces turned her way. The drill man let out a hiss.

"I thought 'ee be a bloody tommyknocker," he said, wiping his brow. "And 'ere I don't believe in no goblins."

The man closest to her laid his hammer against the wall and sat on a rock. He wiped his hands on his red-checkered shirt and scanned the darkness behind her. "The captain be with 'ee?" he asked. The other two men also sat and waited for her answer.

"No," she said. "It's just me."

"Then what 'ee be doing 'ere?" the man asked. "Boy like 'ee don't belong 'ere."

"I'm looking for Matthew Penhallow."

"Well, he ain't 'ere. Best 'ee be home, you. Who let you down?"

Kathy stood mutely, unsure what to say. The red-shirted miner stood up, hitting his head on a black metal candleholder pinned into the wall. He growled as hot wax dripped on his face. "Be gone now, boy. Get 'ee up to grass. This ain't no place for a lad like 'ee, my son."

"But—" Kathy started.

The miner took a menacing step toward her. "Do as 'ee are told. I'd take 'ee there myself if I 'ad the time." He took another step.

"I'll go, I'll go," she said. She turned and scurried into the darkness.

"For 'eavens sake, my son," the miner called after her. "Light a candle."

Stumbling around the rocky bend, Kathy stopped to strike a match, but the flickering light didn't help. She didn't know what to do next. How was she going to find Matthew? She was running out of time. An ache in her head pressed forward. What if she never found him?

"Penhallow, Penhallow." Faded echoes floated along the rocky walls.

Kathy's head snapped up. "Penhallow?" she whispered. "Penhallow?" she said louder, ignoring a new tingling sensation. "Do you know where Matthew Penhallow is?"

A flutter of cold air brushed her face, followed by a scuffing noise. A little man with a large, bulbous nose stepped into the light, the thud of his heavy boots swirling dust onto his blue work pants and sweat-stained shirt. Kathy caught her breath. It was the dwarf from under the porch, only his beard was short and dark, with a coppery sheen, instead of long and gray.

"Penhallow's one level up," he said, walking around her, eyeing her up and down, "by way of the raise."

"The what?" Kathy asked, eyeing the tommyknocker back.

"The raise," he replied. He beckoned for her to follow as he headed down the tunnel. He stopped at a small cubbyhole that Kathy had missed along the way and pointed up a ladder that stretched high into a dark shaft and disappeared. "Up the raise and to your right. Be careful. There is another."

Water trickled out of the darkness and down the rock, soaking the ladder and ground below. Watching her step, Kathy leaned over and gazed up into the darkness. She could see nothing. It was just a black hole. She turned to protest, but the dwarf was gone, leaving her all alone. She stared at the ladder with its slippery wood. What was it David had said? Gritting her teeth with fear and frustration, she grabbed the dripping ladder and placed her shoe on the first slick rung.

Step by step she climbed, as the ladder wobbled underneath. Higher and higher—there seemed no end. Thirty steps up, a sagging rung broke under her foot, forcing her to grip the ladder with both hands. To her horror, her candle slipped through her fingers and tumbled to the depths below. Kathy closed her eyes against the sudden darkness. With a pounding heart, her blood throbbed to panic's pulse, matching the heartbeat of the mountain. Digging her nails into the slippery wood, she opened her eyes and willed herself to take another step. "Please hold," she begged.

She became touch, taste, sound—pain and fear. Arms and legs cried out from constant pushing and pulling, while her jaw ached from clenching teeth. She thought she was doomed to climb forever in a rocky grave. And then a tiny seed of light poked its way through the darkness above, offering life. Kathy climbed faster.

The light grew brighter and at last she saw the top. With relief, she hauled herself out of the shaft onto solid ground. Exhausted, she crawled away from the hole and leaned against the rugged wall. She was in another tunnel. Resting her head on a rock, she closed her eyes and let the rays of flickering light bathe her face with pale warmth. Someone had pinned a candleholder into the stone next to the open raise and left a flame burning. But Kathy had no time to relax. A sudden ache pricked her head, while muted shouting bounced through the darkened tunnel.

"No!" she cried, pushing herself to her feet despite her weary limbs. "I can't be late." She whirled around, trying to orient herself. "To the right, to the right," she babbled as she grabbed a second candle from her pocket, lit it from the flame in the wall, and ran down the tunnel toward the angry noise.

Two men struggled in the light of a candle flickering from a wall where the tunnel forked. Kathy knew them both. Matthew pushed the bigger and stockier Nose away and turned to grasp something in the dirt. While the miner's back was turned, The Nose lifted a large rock from a nearby pile and raised it over his victim's head. Kathy screamed as Matthew looked up and the rock smashed down. The miner crumpled to the ground.

The Nose sneered, his gold tooth glinting in the candlelight. Before Kathy could move, he snatched her arms and threw her to the ground beside Matthew's twitching body. She stared, horrified, into the ravaged face. Her stomach lurched and she felt like throwing up. She hadn't been fast enough. She hadn't arrived in time.

"I know you," The Nose said, knocking the cap off her cropped red hair. "You followed me from Boulder, didn't ya? You and those two boys. Asking lots of questions. Too many questions." He reached for another rock and raised it high to strike. Then he stopped and stared at Matthew's now-still hand. Cupped inside the lifeless fingers, a bronze medallion lay half-hidden under a broken chain. Kathy gasped. It was Matthew's key!

"You can't have it," she yelled, rage replacing fear. She clutched a sharp rock and a fistful of dirt and flung them at the killer's face. Twisting around, she seized the bronze tree of life from Matthew's hand and scrambled to get away. Something hard smashed down on her shoulder, sending bright bolts of pain shooting down her back and arm. The pendant slipped from her fingers.

"This is mine," The Nose snarled as he picked up the medallion and held it in the air. Then he let out an "Oof," and tumbled to the ground. Behind him stood a little man with a large bulbous nose, dark fury on his face. The tommyknocker snatched the pendant and slapped The Nose on the head. Startled, The Nose growled at the dwarf and gathered himself to attack, until he suddenly realized what was standing there, slightly shimmering in the light. He drew back with fear.

The tommyknocker curled his lip, then raised a long, skinny finger and hissed:

> *Through death and greed you taint the sign*
> *that marks the way of a gifted line.*
> *Forever lost the sign will be—*
> *and so will you, if you don't flee.*

He clapped his hands and barked, "Go!"

The Nose let out a strangled cry and fled down the left passageway. The tommyknocker chuckled deep in his throat. "Wrong tunnel," he said. He turned toward Kathy and gave her an odd, speculative look. Then, with a shrug, he walked into the darkness, the pendant swinging from his hand.

"Wait," Kathy cried. She pushed herself up with her uninjured arm. "Wait." Only silence answered. Instinctively, she hollered. "'To save this man you may be late, but more's at stake than one man's fate. It is the key that you must save, don't let me take it to its grave.'" She waited for a response. There was none. "Don't take it to its grave," she yelled. "It's not what you want."

She waited and listened. Then, with a moan, she slumped to the ground. "Now we'll never get home."

"What grave?" the little man asked as he stepped back into the light.

Faster than she could have imagined, Kathy lunged for the man and wrapped all ten fingers around his arm. This time he wouldn't disappear. In an onslaught of words, she told him about the porch and recited the riddle—at least as much as she could remember—while filling in the rest with explanation.

The tommyknocker scratched his bearded chin. "Sounds like me," he said. He looked at the mine around him. "The bal must have been abandoned for it to become a grave. And the pendant never returned." He eyed Kathy sharply. "A porch? The others ruled harshly to banish me there." He shook his head. "I must have hated it."

"I don't really know," Kathy said, "but you wanted us to fix it." She studied the creature before her, marveling at his face, his hands—everything about him. Oddly, she no longer felt afraid. She stretched out her hand. "I'm supposed to take the pendant—the key—and return it to its rightful place."

The little man stroked the medallion with his thumb. "And you know where that is?" he asked, his coal-black eyes twinkling in the light.

"I think so," she replied.

The tommyknocker nodded, then slowly, almost reluctantly, put the pendant in her hand. "Then be gone," he said as he turned away.

"But . . . what about Matthew?" Kathy asked, her throat tightening with grief and loss. But she had no time for tears. "Did I do that? Am I really an omen of death?"

The tommyknocker laughed. "Only to those with foolish minds. Your world believes many things that aren't true—and denies others that are. A fickle world you live in. But then, so is mine." His eyes saddened as he looked over at Matthew. "Penhallow made a grievous mistake—and paid with his life. It is done."

"And The Nose?" Kathy asked, glancing at the passageway where The Nose had fled.

"He killed a man out of greed and darkness in his

heart," the tommyknocker replied. "Into darkness he has gone. He made his own destiny." Suddenly, he cocked his head, listening as agitated whispers rustled in the air. "The fool!" he exclaimed. "He's taken a flame around black powder." He grabbed Kathy's arm:

> *Go now quickly and make haste.*
> *Return the key to its rightful place.*
> *Know in time the gift you bear*
> *by the symbol that you'll wear.*

"What?" Kathy asked, startled.

"Go!" The tommyknocker said, pushing her down the tunnel from whence she had come. "Go *now!*"

The urgency in his voice silenced Kathy's questions. Deep within the earth, an explosive rumble sent shock waves through the rock and air, snuffing out the candles. Clouds of smoke and dust rolled over her as pieces of rock fell and shattered at her feet. She stumbled down the dark tunnel, feeling her way while gripping the pendant in her hand.

She couldn't breathe.

Dust billowed into her lungs, cutting off her air. She pulled her jacket over her mouth and plunged on, banging toes and hands. She turned a corner and saw a hazy light before her. Remembering the pit in the floor, she slowed to a walk.

She found the open shaft by the light of the candle,

its black mouth turned gray in the dusty air. She knew she could never climb down, not with her injured shoulder. Far below, smothered hollering surged up the raise. She turned around in a circle, unsure what to do next. She felt trapped and confused while swirling dust thickened around her.

"Keep going," a voice whispered in her head. She looked down the tunnel in the direction where she had never been. Slipping the pendant in her pocket, she pulled out the last candle and lit it with the dying flame on the wall. Cupping the light in her hand, she ran.

18 Destiny

Kathy crashed down the tunnel. Her heart raced with every step, while dust choked and blinded her and filled her mouth with the taste of death. She kept running.

She almost ran too far.

The flaming wick on the wall saved her. She remembered the raise with its candlelight and stumbled to a halt, right at the edge of the main mineshaft. She had reached the end of the tunnel. There was no place to go but up—or down.

Voices shouted in the hazy depths of the shaft and a flash of black whooshed by as the bucket plummeted down, its cable snaking out behind. The cable jerked to a stop and swung in the air. The voices hushed, followed by a single ping of the signal bell. Slowly, the cable wound its way up. The bucket was rising.

Kathy felt dizzy at the thought of riding in the bucket again, but the idea of climbing a ladder made her want to throw up. She'd never make it. The throbbing pain and stiffness in her shoulder said no to that. But she had to get out of the mountain. Maybe she could get help. She inched toward the lip of the tunnel.

The cable slithered past, creaking under the weight of the bucket. She could see the black form now. She waved and hollered at the men riding up—two standing on the rim and one tucked inside. Startled faces stared out as they passed. Did they see her? Would they get her out?

She leaned into the darkness and looked up, then quickly pulled back, remembering the shards of stone that had followed her down. Curling her good arm around herself and cradling her injured one, she slumped to the ground and sat, throbbing with exhaustion, inside and out. Where were the whispers now?

"Are you there?" she asked. "Will they come back?"

"Patience," whispered the dark.

Three bells rang, then three more, followed by two. The rumble of moving cable and the clang of iron hitting rock showered down the shaft toward her. The bucket was coming down, slowly this time. When it reached her level, the red-shirted miner grabbed the wire cord by the wall and pulled. The bell rang once and the bucket stopped. He stood there, balancing himself on the bucket's rim, and scowled. He was not happy.

"I told 'ee to get to grass," he said. "'Ee could have been killed." He looked at Kathy closely, his scowl turning into surprise. He reached out with his hand. "Let's be going. The bal's not safe."

Kathy stood and reached out with her good arm. The miner grasped her hand and helped her step onto the rim of the bucket, one hand holding her while the other gripped the cable. "'Old tight now."

Briefly letting go of her, he pulled the cord once. The bucket rose. Faster and faster it went as Kathy clung to the cable, grateful for the strong hand on her arm. She still felt dizzy. Without the miner, she knew she would fall. Finally, the bucket slowed, then stopped. Several hands grabbed her and lifted her to solid ground. The fresh, crisp air of night never smelled so good.

"Ain't that the boy I told to git?" one of the ore sorters said.

The red-shirted miner stepped off the bucket. "This be no boy. She be a maid."

Kathy's hand shot to her hair and felt its cropped edges. Her cap still lay on the ground where The Nose had knocked it off. Unhappy faces surrounded her.

"A red-haired woman in the bloody mine."

"'Tis a bad omen, 'tis."

"I bet she blew the mine."

"That's plain foolishness," the red-shirted miner said.

Angry muttering washed back and forth among the men.

"She knows something."

"I bet she's working for the Caribou."

"A red-haired woman in the bloody mine."

Alarmed by the unfriendly glares, Kathy moved

closer to the red-shirted miner. She reached out to touch his arm. "Thanks," she said. Then she bolted for the door.

It must have been her red hair that slowed the men's reactions. Ducking and weaving, she slipped past sluggish hands that reached out to grasp her. Pounding boots rushed after her, until they stopped with a crash and curses. She didn't slow down to look back. She ran down the road as fast as she could, gripping her injured arm to her side. She wasn't fast enough. Footsteps crunched up behind her—and then began to pass. David and Frank waved as they pulled in front and led the way to their hideout.

Kathy's lungs cried for air as she collapsed on the rocky floor. David and Frank both bent over, hands on their knees, trying to catch their breath.

"Did you see the look on that guy's face?" Frank said, grinning. "I told you that tripwire was a great idea."

David tried to giggle through his panting, but coughed instead. When his coughing subsided, he turned to Kathy. "Did you find him? Did you find Matthew?"

Now that she was safe with her brother and Frank, Kathy's face crumpled and she broke into tears.

David and Frank listened while she struggled to tell her story. She didn't want to remember Matthew's face, didn't want to describe the pain. But she did. She shared every detail of the bucket ride, the whispers, and Matthew's death. She showed David the pendant, explaining the symbols as Matthew had. She described her flight from the explosion and the comfort of the whispers as she waited in the dark.

Frank and David asked a few questions, then sat in silence, lost in their separate thoughts. Careful not to jar her arm, Kathy stroked the pendant in her hand, tracing the tree of life with her finger. The embers of the dying fire burned lower and lower, then suddenly dimmed out as a draft blew through the cave, carrying a whisper.

"Go now quickly and make haste, return the key to its rightful place."

Frank jumped to his feet. "Cripes, what's that?"

"It's that dwarf, again," David cried, reaching for his sister's arm. "Come on. Let's get out of here."

Kathy protested and turned toward the inner depths of the abandoned mine, but both boys grabbed her arms and hauled her to her feet. Ignoring her cries of pain, they pushed her out into the open air, then staggered to a halt. Spread before them in the warm night air was a manicured lawn, street lights, and paved streets. They turned and gaped at the red-shingled house with its porch and sandstone wall. The door under the porch hung open.

Kathy didn't know whether to laugh or cry. Frank just stood there with a grin on his face, while David whooped and hollered.

"Shh," Kathy whispered, "you're going to wake someone up and get us into trouble." She walked back to the doorway and peered in. "Do you think he's still there?"

"I don't know, but we're not going to find out," David said, pulling at his sister's arm. "Come on."

She resisted the tug and shook him loose. She stood a moment longer, staring into the darkness. Then, with a grunt, she pushed the wooden door shut, its rusty hinges screeching into the night. "You're right," she said, turning to look her brother in the eye. "Because we're not done yet." Holding her head high, she marched across the grass to the sidewalk.

"Wait," Frank said, eyeing the door. "What about my shoes and jacket?"

"Forget them," Kathy replied, moving down the street. The riddle wasn't finished and she didn't want to waste any time.

"Mom's going to kill me," Frank groaned from somewhere behind. Boots clicked on the flagstone sidewalk as he or David or both hurried to catch up. Kathy didn't bother to look back. She had a job to do. She had just reached the end of the Elberts' yard when a tiny *screak* cut through the air. Kathy lurched to a stop.

"Frank, we don't have time," she said loudly as she whirled around and bumped into David. Frank sidestepped the collision with an annoyed look on his face.

"What?" he said.

Kathy blinked at the two boys and then glanced at the porch, now hidden in shadow. A breeze stirred the air, knocking branches together. "Nothing," she said. She started down the street again and the boys folllowed.

She led them back the way they had come, four days and more than a hundred years ago: past the houses; past the schoolyard; past her own house with the black iron fence. She went straight to Mrs. Acheson's house and up the porch steps that glowed from the light shining through the window. She reached out with her uninjured arm and rang the bell.

The door opened and Mrs. Acheson stood in the light. A flour-spattered apron covered her calico dress.

"You're up a bit late, aren't you?" she asked, as her face crinkled into a smile. She looked at their dirty clothes and *tsk*ed. "Where have you three been? You smell like you haven't bathed for days." A suspicious look spread over her face. "You haven't been searching more garbage bins, have you? Because if you have, there are a lot more weeds in my garden than those you plucked out this afternoon."

"Gosh, no," Kathy said. "We didn't do that. We've been . . . well . . . here," she said, handing the pendant to her neighbor.

Mrs. Acheson examined the medallion in her hand, a puzzled look on her face. She turned the bronze disc over and traced its design. Her face shifted from confusion to disbelief and then surprise.

"Is this what I think it is?" she asked.

"It belonged to Matthew—Matthew Penhallow," Kathy said. "I believe it belongs to you now."

"The key," Mrs. Acheson whispered as she held

the pendant up in the light. "How did you . . . ?" She cleared her throat, then stood aside. "Inside," she said briskly, waving Kathy and the boys through the door. "I want to hear *all* about it."

"Could we get something to eat?" Frank asked, as he trudged into the house with Mrs. Acheson's finger poking him in the back to hurry. "Something other than peaches?"

"I think I can handle that," Mrs. Acheson said as she slipped the medallion into her apron pocket and disappeared down the hall.

Cradling her arm, Kathy sat on the sofa in the small living room while David and Frank sprawled in large, cushioned chairs. Kathy couldn't help but smile at the yellow foxgloves that overflowed in porcelain vases scattered throughout the room. Maybe she could write a poem about them.

It wasn't long before Mrs. Acheson returned with a tray of steaming-hot blueberry muffins. She placed the tray on the coffee table in front of the sofa, pushing aside an opened photo album and several old photographs that were scattered by the album's side. Frank reached for the nearest muffin and took an enormous bite.

Clasping her hands behind her back, Mrs. Acheson stood in the center of the room and raised an eyebrow at the trio. "Now then, let's begin."

Kathy, Frank, and David looked at each other, mouths

clamped shut. Finally, Kathy took a deep breath. "We went ghost hunting," she said. "That's where it all started."

The trio spent the next hour telling everything they could remember, right up to knocking on Mrs. Acheson's door. Mrs. Acheson grunted and nodded, never once questioning the validity of what they said. When they mentioned James, surprise flickered over her face, but she didn't say a word. At last the story was finished and Kathy, David, and Frank fell silent. Mrs. Acheson sighed.

"Great-grandmother wondered what happened to the pendant," she said. "Her husband, Matthew, died in a mine explosion, or so she was told, but when the miners found him, the pendant was missing. My great-grandmother always suspected foul play." Mrs. Acheson pulled the medallion out of her pocket and stroked it with her fingers. "But the key has been found and there is a new babe on the way. Perhaps my grandniece's child will have the gift."

"But Kathy has. . . . Ow!" Frank cried, as David kicked him in the shin.

Mrs. Acheson chuckled. "Yes, I suspect she might, but a key belongs to a family line and this must stay in mine."

Kathy looked at the bronze medallion, feeling a sense of loss. "What does it do?" she asked softly, rubbing at the ache in her arm.

"It opens doors between two worlds," Mrs. Acheson replied. "Doors shut by disbelief and neglect. A gifted person can find the open doors, more so than the common man, and sometimes push them wider, but only a key can unlock doors that have been shut." She walked over to the mantle above the fireplace. Gently she laid the pendant next to a picture frame with a brown, faded map inside.

Kathy's mouth dropped open. "You have the map."

"My great-grandfather's copy, yes," Mrs. Acheson said. "There were two copies, you know. With the pendant, the map is complete. See? You place the pendant here, over this mark, and let the birds point the way—a thousand feet by blackbird's wings, four hundred feet by nightly owl." She traced a line on the map with her finger and then tapped a spot. "That's where the vein of ore lies."

"Does that mean we're going to be rich?" Frank asked.

Mrs. Acheson laughed and pointed her finger at the map. "That's what created all the trouble in the first place, am I right?"

Frank nodded.

Mrs. Acheson fixed emerald-green eyes on Kathy. "The gift is not to be used for greed—only to serve others' needs. Besides," she said, looking at Frank, "those U.S. geology boys found the vein last year. That mountain is crawling with people now."

"Figures," Frank said as he reached for another muffin. He stopped and stared open-mouthed at a faded photograph on the coffee table. "Who's that?" he asked, pointing to the brown- and cream-colored photo of a young man and woman sitting stiffly in old-fashioned clothes. The woman held a young child on her lap.

Mrs. Acheson chuckled. "They're my grandparents, James and Emily Reskelly, and my mother when she was a baby," she replied. "James married Emily, Matthew's daughter."

"Yes!" Frank cried, jumping to his feet. "James is okay. He didn't die."

"I would certainly hope not," Mrs. Acheson said, her eyes twinkling with amusement. "I wouldn't be here if he had."

Frank could barely contain his excitement. He hopped for joy in the middle of the room. Kathy grinned at his antics, then leaned over for a closer look at the picture. Now that Mrs. Acheson had pointed it out, she recognized James's and Emily's faces. Was there a picture of Matthew, too? She reached out to pull the album toward her but stopped midway, wincing at the pain in her shoulder.

"Let me see that," Mrs. Acheson said, hurrying to Kathy's side. Gently poking and prodding, she examined Kathy's back and shoulder. "Just bruised, I imagine. Nasty one, though. Go home and get some rest. We'll talk more tomorrow."

David took his sister's hand. "Come on, Kath. You can shower first."

Frank, David, and Kathy left Mrs. Acheson waving good-night in the doorway. They walked back to the black gate in front of the Henley house. Frank stuck his hands in his jeans pockets and shuffled awkwardly. "I'll see you guys tomorrow, huh?"

"Sure," David replied, as he unlatched the gate and pushed it open.

Frank stood there, waiting. Kathy smiled and nodded. "Tomorrow," she said.

Frank grinned, then waved goodbye. He strode down the street, tossing a marble into the air while whistling a Western tune.

Inside, Kathy let the warm water wash over her, cleaning every scrape and cut and massaging her bruised and aching muscles. Lathering her hands, she shampooed her hair, trying to ignore the shortness of its locks. She avoided the mirror as she brushed her teeth and scrubbed away four days of fuzz. Then, wrapping her terry cloth robe around her, she opened the door to David's room. He was sitting on his bed, examining a rock.

"Did it really happen?" Kathy asked, as she leaned against the doorjamb. "Now that I'm clean, it all feels like a dream. I don't even have the pendant any more."

"Sure it happened," David replied. "For one thing, you've got a bruise the size of a cantaloupe on your back and, well, you lost a lot of hair. For another, I've still got this smelly coat. But," he added, "I've also got this rock." He held up the fist-sized rock in his hand. Kathy could see an inch-wide streak of gray running through the middle. David grinned. "There's silver in them thar hills."

"You didn't."

"I didn't," David replied. "One of the miners gave it to me. Frank asked so many questions, the miner gave us each one to shut us up. I think Frank dropped his when he rigged the tripwire, but he didn't much care. Prefers the marble, I guess." He put the rock on his bookshelf next to a large quartz crystal. "Now go to bed," he said, waving Kathy through the bathroom. "My turn for a shower."

Kathy walked into her room and pulled on her over-sized T-shirt. She started to throw her dirty clothes into the laundry basket when she remembered the paper stuffed in her denim jacket. Carefully, she pulled out the picture of an owl sitting in the branches of an old pine tree and smiled at the message scribbled below. She had a greater treasure from their journey than a marble or a rock.

She slipped the picture into her sketchpad with the knobby-nosed chestnut tree and placed the pad back on the bookshelf, next to her pencils and the picture of her Grandmother Faye. Then, exhausted, she crawled into the soft folds of her sheets and blanket, ignoring the crumpled heap of dirty clothes on the floor and not caring that the closet door was open. As she drifted off to sleep, she heard a whisper float through her window like a comforting melody.

> *Know in time the gift you bear*
> *by the symbol that you'll wear.*

When Kathy awoke, bright sunshine filled the room, the morning chill long gone. Careful of her shoulder, she crawled out of bed. She reached for her hairbrush on the nightstand and stopped. A folded note in her mother's pink stationery rested on top of a small white box, carefully sealed shut with a daub of burgundy wax on each side. Kathy picked up the note, opened it, and read.

Dear Kathy,

David said you were up late last night reading, so I thought I'd let you sleep. Grandmother Faye left you this box in her will. She wanted you to have it on your twelfth birthday, first thing, when you awoke.

Happy birthday, dear!

Love, Mom

Kathy put down the note and picked up the box. She broke its seals with her finger and lifted the top. Inside, a delicate silver chain curled on top of a golden-bronze disc. Gently, Kathy picked up the pendant and turned it over. In the center of a tangled circle of knots were the arching boughs of the tree of life, with an eagle, a blackbird, and an owl.

Historical notes

Not everyone knows what it is like to crawl under a porch looking for a little old man. I do. When I was young, a neighbor dared me to brave the spiders and the dark. We never found anyone, but I always wondered—what if we had?

Riddle in the Mountain is a work of fiction, but the story also contains many elements based on history. Boulder, Nederland, and Caribou are real places. Today Boulder is a thriving city, Nederland is a tourist-destination mountain town, and Caribou has become a ghost town with little left to see. In Boulder, there is still a house with a sandstone wall and a chestnut tree in the back yard, as well as a shaggy-shingled house with a porch you can crawl under.

In taking Kathy, Frank, and David back in time, I tried to be as historically accurate as possible about the existence and location of buildings, in describing typical daily events, and in depicting the general living conditions. The Stone Barn, Brainard Hotel, and Belvidere House were well-known Boulder landmarks in 1879. The Caribou stage stopped at the Nederland House on its way to Caribou. Sprawling down the banks of Boulder Creek, the Nederland Mill crunched rock to extract ore dug out of local mines, including the No Name and Caribou mines in Caribou. In 1879, Rocky Mountain Joe, Annie Brainard, George Bottoms, and Mr. Simpson lived and worked in the Boulder community, while boys with nothing better to do splattered carriages with wads of mud and rigged tripwires along the uneven boardwalks.

Many other events depicted in the story did not actually occur but were typical of the times. There never was a fire at the Stone Barn, although livery fires, as well as house fires, were not unusual and firemen did have to pull their own wagons to reach the burning buildings. Freighting accidents also were common in the Rocky Mountain West. The road up Boulder Canyon was steep and often treacherous—like most rough mountain roads. It took skilled freighters to safely deliver goods to and from the mining camps, but skill was not always enough to guarantee safety.

Perhaps my favorite place in the story is the town of Caribou, not only because of the Cornish miners, who played an important role in opening the West, but because of my own memories of the place. When I was young and my family visited the ghost town of Caribou, little remained of the once thriving community: a few skeletal shacks sagging from years of neglect; mine pits gaping open in the ground; and, its image still clear in my mind, the Caribou cemetery.

At that time, several marble headstones still rose out of the ground in the cemetery, some encircled by small wrought-iron fences. Today, not a single stone remains. As in many mountain cemeteries, thoughtless visitors stole or destroyed those remaining headstones that had survived nearly a century of wind, rain, and snow.

Still, I vividly remember one of those vanished markers: a four-sided obelisk, standing perhaps three feet high. On three of its sides the name of a child was engraved: Anna Richards, Willie Richards, and Alice May Richards. These three young people died within a four-day period during the diphtheria epidemic that swept through the community in 1879. It is in their honor that I set *Riddle in the Mountain* in that year.

Rocky Mountain Joe

As I began to research this book, discovering the life of Rocky Mountain Joe was like finding a nugget of gold. He looked like the perfect frontiersman and he had lived a fascinating life. I was as intrigued as Kathy became in *Riddle.* He warmed his way into our hearts.

Joseph Bevier Sturtevant was born in 1851 and spent much of his young life in Wisconsin, where his father traded with the Indians. As mentioned in the story, he apprenticed to a broom-maker, then ran away to join the circus. When the Civil War broke out, Joe joined the 4th Wisconsin Cavalry. He fought in Alabama and Louisiana, then left the cavalry in 1863 and headed to the Dakotas because of conflicts involving the Sioux and the Cheyenne. Captured twice during the Indian Wars, Joe managed to escape both times. He then served as a scout for a brief time, before finally settling in Boulder, Colorado, where he earned his nickname. In his buckskin clothing and with his knowledge of the outdoors, he looked like someone who should be called *Rocky Mountain Joe.*

In Boulder, Joe initially worked at hanging wallpaper and painting houses, but in 1884 he discovered photography. He is most remembered for this skill. We still depend on the invaluable record his photographs provide of life in the nineteenth-century Rocky Mountains, and of the Boulder area's history between 1884 and 1910, the year of his death.

The Cornish in America

With the discovery of gold in California and later in the Rocky Mountains, men from every walk of life and many different countries swarmed into the Western frontier to seek their fortune. Any man and every man—almost all the prospectors were men—could pan for the gold that could be found in streambeds or found lying on the ground. Farmers, tailors, shopkeepers, and others abandoned their former lives. Panning for gold required little money or skill.

However, an even greater treasure lay deep below the surface, where veins of mineral ore threaded their way through mountain stone. But extracting this hidden wealth was a tricky business called hard-rock mining. Mines were dangerous, difficult, and expensive to build. Hard-rock mining wasn't suited for any fortune-seeker who packed up his bags and left home. It required skilled, experienced miners who understood blasting, timbering, hoisting, flooding, and ventilating, men who could wield hammers and drills as if they were born with the tools in their hands. It required men like the Cornish.

Cornwall is in the farthest southwestern corner of England, on the tip of a large peninsula that divides the English

Channel on the south from the Celtic Sea on the north. Here, the Cornish had been mining tin since prehistoric times and had mined underground since the fifteenth century. By the 1800s, they were ranked among the world's greatest hard-rock miners. In *A History of American Mining*, Thomas Rickard said that Cornishmen "knew better than anyone how to break rock, how to timber bad ground, and how to make the other fellow shovel it, tram it and hoist it."[1]

Drawn to opportunities in the New World, many Cornish men and women immigrated to the mining frontiers of North America and settled in Pennsylvania, Michigan, Wisconsin, Illinois, Montana, South Dakota, Arizona, Utah, Nevada, California, and Colorado. Called *Cousin Jacks* and *Cousin Jennies* in the new territories, they brought with them words like *shaft, winze, raise, adits,* and *levels,* now standard mining terms. The miner's candlestick and lunch pail came from Cornwall, along with the Cornish pump, the horse whim, and the mining-bell signals. The Cornish brought expertise and an eye for innovations. They also brought their culture.

Many old mining communities contained "Cousin Jack" stories poking fun at the distinctive Cornish dialect, but the Cornish are also remembered for their caroling, their brass and silver bands, and their general love of music. Out of their strong faith, mostly Methodist, these people formed communities with social and religious stability, in contrast to many unruly mining towns. They enlivened holidays with wrestling matches and drilling contests, and they introduced *pasties, saffron cake, herby pie, figgy pudden,* and *kiddle broth* to American palates.

Mining Folklore

Like the miners, mining folklore in early America came from a variety of ethnic origins. The Cornish brought with them the *tommyknocker* or *knocker,* as it was called in Cornwall, a small,

[1]Thomas A. Rickard, *A History of American Mining* (New York: McGraw-Hill, 1932), page 248.

dwarf-like creature who worked in the mines. The Cornish viewed tommyknockers as relatively friendly and helpful. The knockers often warned miners of cave-ins, and on occasion would lead a miner to a rich vein of ore. They could be vindictive, however, if neglected or abused through disrespect. Many miners left bits of lunch behind for the tommyknockers, as a courtesy.

Similar in appearance but otherwise unlike the tommyknocker, the German *kobold* was a sinister mine-dwelling creature. Kobolds would deliberately cause cave-ins and lead miners into dangerous situations. *Step-devils*, dwarfish creatures with long arms that reached to the ground, came from Mexican and Native American folklore. During times of disaster, a step-devil would pull himself up a ladder, destroying the rungs or foot-notches as he went, thus trapping the miners below.

Because mines were such dangerous places and luck played a large role in the miners' well-being, a great deal of lore developed around signs of luck, especially bad luck. Whistling in a mine was thought to drive away the "good luck spirits." Women in or near a mine were considered bad luck, perhaps because historically women only came to the mines in times of tragedy, looking for lost loved ones. Dropping tools or having clothes fall from a locker or hook was thought to foretell the owner's fall down a shaft, or a similar mishap. When men were traveling to the mine, a dog's howling or a black cat's crossing the pathway was considered an ill omen. Likewise, seeing a snail on the way to work was a bad sign. But in this case a remedy was at hand: the miner could drop a bit of candle tallow or leave a crumb of lunch for the snail and go on his way.

On the other hand, rats and mice were welcome sights in the mine. Miners left crumbs for the rodents and frequently gave them names. To kill a rat was taboo, for these creatures seemed to sense when a cave-in or other mishap was about to happen and warned the miners by leaving the area. As the saying went, "When rats move out, so does the miner."

Acknowledgments

Writing a book set in the historic West is like mining for gold and silver: you dig here, tap there, and in the end take the big plunge. This book could not have been completed without a lot of moral support and expert advice.

I would like to thank my writers' group, the Sage Writers' Cache, for enduring many drafts of the manuscript. In particular, I would like to thank Judy Fort Brenneman, Deborah Robson, and Rebekah Robson-May, who have read and critiqued the book not once, not twice, but many times.

In addition, Rita Ritchie played an instrumental role in getting me through my first few drafts, while Q Pearson and Barbara Steiner provided helpful feedback on later drafts.

In exploring the past, I have been fortunate to have been able to consult a wealth of experts. I would like to thank David L. Newell of the Colorado Historical Society and the Costume Society of America for clarifying the dress styles in the 1870s and checking my clothing accuracy; Silvia Pettem for her extensive knowledge of historic Boulder and Boulder County; Caroline Nordyke for providing me with pointers on driving horses and mules; Tom Hendricks of the Caribou Mine for bringing hard-rock mining to life; Harrison Cobb for reviewing Kathy's adventures inside the mine; Greta Penrose Erm for tapping into her Cornish roots to help with customs and dialect; C. W. Sullivan III for sharing his knowledge of Celtic folklore; and the folks on the mining-history list-serve, who helped me understand the difference between a winze and a raise.

Finally, I would like to thank Frank Riccio for bringing his magic to the pages of the book and all of my family for encouraging me in this endeavor. I offer special thanks to my parents, Don and Dorine Burkhard, who not only cheered me on but gave me the blessing of time.

—*Daryl Burkhard*

Notes on the typefaces

The main text is set in Bitstream Arrus, designed by Richard Lipton (Bitstream, 1991). It's set 10/15 for the body of the book and 9/12 for the notes. The title on the cover and the chapter titles are in Niederwald, a typeface based on nineteenth-century hand-lettered signs from the Western United States, by Dave Nalle (Scriptorium, 1993). The type in the dedication and in Kathy's mother's letter is Rodeo Girl BV, by Jess Latham (Blue Vinyl Fonts, 2003). Lachesis appears in various locations (including the headings in the historical notes and acknowledgments; the newspaper date on page 58; and the initial caps on the historical notes, acknowledgments, and this page). Lachesis also has roots in the late nineteenth century and was designed by Dave Nalle (Scriptorium, 1993). The running heads are TF Arrow Book Italic, by Joseph Treacy (Treacyfaces). The decorative images come from Alien Ornaments, by Amondó Szegi (T26, 2000); P22 Woodcut Extras, by Richard Kegler (P22, 1996); and TF Neue Neuland Ornaments, by Joseph Treacy (Treacyfaces). Thanks to all the type designers: their work makes for enjoyable layout and pleasant reading.